THE DRUM

E.E. BURKE

Cover Design by Erin Dameron-Hill

Published by E.E. Burke
ISBN 9780998071299

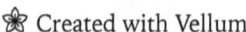 Created with Vellum

PROLOGUE

OCTOBER 1876, NOELLE, COLORADO

*T*he door to the Hardt & Co. office swung open, and a wiry bow-legged miner in dusty denims stepped inside. He snatched off his cap and tugged a lock of his hair. "Mornin' Mr. Hardt, sir. Would ye mind writing up a pretty letter? Somethin' ta woo a bride?"

Charlie glanced up from the account book spread out in front of him. Silas Powell's request to have a letter written wasn't particularly surprising, as many of the mine employees were illiterate and asked for their employer's help with letters. But a request to *woo a bride* was a new one. "Am I getting married? That's mighty odd. Nobody told me."

Confusion flashed across Silas's face an instant before a grin appeared, indicating the miner had caught on to the deliberate misunderstanding. "Too late, sir. There ain't any women left for you to take. They all got assigned, and I already heard back from mine."

So, even a skirt-chaser like Silas had bought into the mail-order bride scheme cooked up by the well-meaning reverend. Chase Hammond had spun a pretty story if he'd convinced hard-bitten miners to give up their fancy whores in exchange for whey-faced wives. Who else would come out to the middle of nowhere and marry strangers?

"Let's talk about this bride." Charlie motioned the miner forward, glad for something to distract from work he hated, especially when the calculations didn't favor him—at the moment. He pushed aside an unopened envelope, which he knew contained another bid to buy him out. He wasn't interested, no matter how many times Percy stuck an offer under his nose.

He leaned back in his chair and stretched to relieve the tightness in his back and arms. "So, Mr. Powell, tell me about how you managed to get hornswoggled into marriage. I heard y'all had to draw straws. Were you one of the unlucky ones?"

The smile on Powell's face faltered and his expression clouded with concern. "What d'ye mean by that, sir? How's it unlucky?"

Charlie shook his head. Miners were a superstitious lot, and he knew better than to joke about something they took very seriously. "Never mind. I'm sure your bride will turn out to be very lucky for you."

Which was more than Charlie could say about *his* former wife.

Silas heaved a relieved sigh. "Aye, I need all the luck I can get."

"Don't we all?" Charlie restrained the urge to warn his worker against marrying a stranger. What did it matter? He'd known Olivia for years and hadn't once guessed the depths of her deception, or else he'd ignored the signs because her beauty had enthralled him. Loveliness on the outside didn't guarantee the same on the inside—in fact, the opposite seemed to be true. Pretty women were more inclined to be self-centered and faithless. For Silas's sake, he hoped the miner got one of the ugly ones.

Charlie pulled a sheet of paper in front of him. Just because he'd sworn off marriage didn't mean others wouldn't benefit, and the town *had* struck a deal with the railroad to have twelve couples married by January sixth. As mayor, he had an obligation to fulfill. The least he could do was help one of his own men land a bride, if that's what he wanted. "Tell me, does your heart's desire have a name?"

"Mrs. Penelope Jackson. She's a widow lady. She sent a picture with her letter." Silas pulled a cabinet card from his coat. The glee in his eyes could only mean he'd been dealt a winning hand.

Unable to resist a peek, Charlie took the card. The *widow lady* wasn't anywhere close to ugly, or even all that old. The woman in the picture had the kind of quiet beauty that reminded him of peaceful mountain streams and breezes fluttering through the aspens.

"I got the prettiest one," Silas declared, with apt reverence.

"To be sure." Charlie's voice came out rougher than intended. He rubbed his thumb over the image and could almost feel the silkiness of her alabaster cheek and the softness of the dark strands escaping an upsweep of loose curls. Her posture and expression bespoke solemn dignity, but the gifted photographer had captured the hopeful longing in her eyes. What was Penelope Jackson hoping for?

He turned the card face down on the desk. Beautiful women were experts at making their eyes say things they didn't really mean. Not to mention, this woman belonged to Silas Powell, or would, as soon as she agreed to marry him.

Charlie lifted his pen out of the inkwell and began to write.

"Dear Mrs. Jackson..."

When Silas didn't say anything, Charlie glanced up, frowning. "What do you want me to say to her?"

The miner's lean cheeks colored. "I don't know. Thought you could, you know, come up with somethin' pretty. You got a smooth way with words."

Charlie frowned. *Smooth words.* That's what had gotten him into trouble the last time, when he had wooed a woman he should've avoided. But that was in the past, along with the mistakes he'd made. For the miner's sake, he'd write a persuasive letter, and then he'd put this behind him too.

Bending to the task, he read aloud as he wrote, knowing Silas couldn't read any better than he could write.

"My employee, Mr. Silas Powell, asked me to pen this letter on his behalf, as he doesn't believe his own words to be worthy enough to sway a lady of your obvious beauty and charm."

"Um, couldn't you just act like *I'm* the one doin' the writing?"

Charlie lifted the pen. Over the years, he'd besmirched his honor in just about every way possible. In all that time, no matter how broke or desperate he'd become, he had never lied. "That wouldn't be honest."

Silas wrung the cap in his hands and uncertainty twisted his features. "She might not like me if she don't think I can read or write."

"Best you know that sooner versus later. Take my word for it; you want a woman who'll accept you as you are, not as she thinks you ought to be. She'll find out your secrets, so it's best to be truthful up front."

The miner looked unconvinced. "If you say so. But you can tell her I'm English, not Irish. I'm only Irish on me mam's side."

"Mr. Powell is of English and Irish descent…" Charlie sized up the miner. *"Brown hair, brown eyes, an average height, but uncommonly strong for his slim build."* That should be enough about how Silas looked. Other things mattered more.

"He is one of my best employees, always the first to show up for work and the last to leave, and he fills in for the other miners when one is sick or injured. The younger men look up to him."

The facts were correct. No reason to add that Silas only worked the extra hours if he was guaranteed twice the pay, or that he was prone to bragging. Everyone had flaws.

"Mr. Powell is a man of integrity." Charlie made eye contact with his employee after he read the last line. His own integrity was at stake if Silas didn't live up to the admirable description.

The prominent Adam's apple in the miner's throat moved as he swallowed. "Thank ye, sir. I have been honest in most things. In all my dealings with you," he added quickly.

Which was to say, he was as honest a man as one could hope to find in the minefields, which were overrun with cheats and liars.

Charlie redirected his attention to the letter. What more could he say that would appeal to a woman of quality and assure her she was making the right decision?

"You may want to know something of our fine town. Noelle, as its name implies, is a town filled with promise and possibilities. Hardworking men like Mr. Powell have made our community what it is today, but what they need are wives who will be loving helpmates and trusted partners. In return, the men will be dependable husbands."

"Mr. Powell is the foreman of the largest mine in the area, which has a promising future as more gold is discov-

ered. Thus far, we've pulled out enough gold to run a successful mining operation"—which wasn't a lie. Up until recently, the mine had been quite successful —*"and have built homes and a dozen places of business, where ladies can find whatever they need to set up a household."*

Silas pursed his lips as he counted on his fingers. "Ain't there more than a dozen?"

"She doesn't need a precise count that includes the saloons and cathouses."

The miner rubbed at the bristle on his chin, looking thoughtful. "You could include The Golden Nugget. It's the nicest saloon in town."

"She's a lady, she won't be impressed by a saloon."

"She would be if she could see the bar."

Perhaps the widow would be impressed by Jack Peregrine's carpentry skills, although it wasn't Jack who needed to impress her. "I'll mention our plans for a school and church. Mrs. Jackson will appreciate knowing that we have higher aspirations than just digging gold out of the ground."

"What's higher than gold?"

"Self-restraint, for one…something you need to practice before she gets here." Charlie reached for the cabinet card, the temptation to look at it again being too great.

Silas got to it first, however, and took it up to examine it. "Is she rich, do you think?"

Clearly, he wasn't overly concerned with higher aspirations.

"Why would a rich woman come out here to marry a stranger?"

"She might be lonely," Silas mused. "Or maybe she wants a change of scenery."

Noises from a commotion outside bled through the oilpaper tacked over the window. The glass had been busted out a week ago when one miner threw another one through it. Based on the tenor and volume of the curses and shouts, another fight appeared to have broken out again.

Charlie knew it would be a waste of time to try to stop the brawl. He considered what more to add. He couldn't write about the frequent brawls, drinking, gambling or whoring. Not if he wanted to help Silas win his bride. "I'll put in a few lines about the scenery."

The vast wonder of God's creation is all around. Mountain lakes are as blue as the sky, and at night, the stars so plentiful, you can reach up and take a handful out of the sky. Or so it seems. The streams are clear, the water pure, the air is sweet and scented with spruce. It can get cold up here, so you should pack warm clothing. Though our doctor tells me that cold weather, if one is dressed for it, can be good for strengthening the blood. We have timber for building and plentiful wildlife to hunt for food. Truly, we have almost everything we need. What we lack are ladies who can polish our rough edges and bring a gentle, civilized touch to our beloved town.

Charlie read back over the final lines he'd written, then, satisfied, looked up at Silas. "That ought to do it. Oh, one more thing. You need to ask for her hand."

"Mr. Powell's fondest hope is that you will accept his proposal and become his wife upon your arrival. He looks forward to your reply. Respectfully, Charles A. Hardt, on behalf of Silas Powell, who offers his fond regards."

Silas flashed a pleased grin. "Thank ye, Mr. Hardt. That's a fine letter."

He waited patiently while Charlie blotted the ink, folded the paper and then slipped it into an envelope. The miner tucked both the letter and the cabinet card inside his coat and patted it. "She's sure to accept me after she reads this."

The prospect of helping Silas find happiness should've improved Charlie's mood. Instead, it sent him further into the doldrums. He suddenly thought of something that might help, or at least it would take his mind off the woman Powell would soon marry.

Charlie pulled out a bottle of whiskey he kept on hand for special occasions. "We'll drink a toast to your upcoming marriage and your pretty bride. May she bring you luck."

CHAPTER 1

JANUARY 4, 1876, NOELLE, COLORADO, THE
11TH DAY OF CHRISTMAS

*P*enny tightened her grip on a simple bouquet of evergreen tied with white ribbon. She took a deep breath, which came out as a white cloud before she opened the door to the saloon and stepped inside.

Barely past dawn and already a few locals had taken their places around the tables to play cards and drink whiskey. A mere two weeks ago, she would never have entered such an establishment. However, in this mining community—her new home—The

Golden Nugget was the only building large enough to house public events such as weddings.

Imagine it's a grand church.

She set off across the room with a stately stride, pretending not to notice the images of naked women hanging above the bar, or the monstrous collection of hides and antlers mounted on the log walls. Looking through a sheer, rose-patterned lace, which covered her face, helped with the illusion.

The wedding party had gathered in the far corner, near a sparsely decorated spruce, leaning slightly off-kilter on its base. Conspicuously absent from the gathering, the most important member besides her —the groom.

"He'll be here," the woman at Penny's side assured her. Birdie Peregrine, who seven days earlier had wed a devoted family man, wore a bright, hopeful expression. The talented French-Canadian seamstress had made Penny's veil, which was supposed to bring good luck.

If only…

Two bearded men in dirty denims eyed her with suspicion as she passed.

"That'uns bad luck," one said under his breath.

"Aye, Silas fears for his life," his companion replied in a hushed tone.

Penny's breathing hitched. *Silas? Her intended?*

Birdie threw the men a scowl before turning back to Penny. "Pay them no mind, they're drunk."

"At this hour?" Penny leaned down to whisper in Birdie's ear. "What if they're right? A few days ago when Mr. Powell came into town, we were walking together when a chunk of ice fell off the roof and struck him on the top of his head. Dr. Deane had to stitch up a very ugly gash."

Birdie lifted one shoulder in a typically Gallic shrug. "Pieces of ice fall off the eaves all the time. He was in the wrong place."

"But three days before that, I slipped on a slick spot and knocked him into a horse trough."

"Those streets are treacherous. He should've visited you indoors."

Penny worried her lower lip. Her groom might still be put out about his broken tooth. The day she'd arrived in Noelle, along with the eleven other mail-order brides, a snowstorm had nearly stranded them on the side of a mountain. Once in town, they'd been shocked by the rough conditions and even rougher greeting they'd received.

She hadn't meant to knock that glass of whiskey into Mr. Powell's front teeth. The mayor, who'd been throttling the preacher at the time, had inadvertently bumped into her. Mr. Hardt had apologized and offered her a handkerchief, which she intended to return today. Not only was her intended absent, but the tall, fair-haired mine owner didn't appear to be in attendance either. Was it possible he and his foreman had both forgotten the wedding?

Despite the cold, a droplet of perspiration slipped beneath Penny's corset. Only she and Agatha, an elderly woman who'd hoped to land a spry husband, remained unmarried. Mr. Powell had seemed willing enough, at first, but she had put off the wedding after their awkward first meeting, wanting to have time to get to know him better. A few days ago, he'd sent word he would be too busy to come to town again before their nuptials. He might've decided to make *her* wait now.

The other ladies greeted her with hugs and strained smiles.

Genevieve Walters, the intrepid matchmaker, took a brisk step forward and clasped Penny's hand with exuberance. "Good morning, my dear. You look lovely."

"A vision," added Reverend Hammond.

If she was such a catch, why hadn't her groom seen fit to be here to cast the net?

Penny glanced worriedly over her shoulder. After being twice widowed, she hadn't intended to marry again, although it hadn't taken much to be talked into giving marriage another try. Her yearning for love had overcome most of her doubts.

"The perfect man is out there," Genevieve had assured her.

The letter she carried next to her heart had convinced her she'd finally found him. Now, she wasn't so sure.

A flurry of feathers appeared from the side of her vision. The Thorntons' pet goose was on the loose again. This had become such a common occurrence it no longer alarmed her, or anyone else for that matter. Flapping and squawking, the bird dashed behind the tree, making the ornaments on the branches sway, including a painted gray and white goose.

Over each of the past ten days, a new ornament had magically appeared on the tree—gifts from a secretive Santa. Penny searched the branches, wondering what he'd left for her on this day, her wedding day?

The door banged behind her, jerking her attention away from the tree.

Silas?

She twisted to look, only to be blasted in the face by an icy wind that swirled into the room.

A man bundled from head to toe stepped inside. As he unwound his scarf, he had to leap out of the way to avoid stepping on the runaway goose when it made a dash for freedom.

Penny released the breath she was holding. *Woody Burnside.* Woody—who also worked for Mr. Hardt, caring for the livestock owned by the mining company—scanned the room as if looking for someone. When his gaze found Penny, his anxious expression saddened. "Silas—I mean, Mr. Powell is…well, he's gone."

Penny tightened her grip on the bouquet so she wouldn't drop it. Beneath the heavy bombazine and layers of petticoats, her skin grew cold and clammy.

"Gone?" Genevieve echoed.

"What do you mean, 'he's *gone?*'" Reverend Hammond demanded.

"Just a while ago, he took one of the horses and rode out of town." Woody answered.

"He fled from *her,*" someone whispered.

Penny's burning cheeks were the only part of her with any feeling left. Her limbs had frozen, and inside she'd gone numb. Hadn't she been warned something like this would happen? Last night, awful nightmares had disturbed what little sleep she'd gotten. She'd dreamed of being lost and wandering alone in the darkness.

The gamblers who were sitting at the tables turned back to their card game, and the miners standing around the room looked everywhere but in Penny's direction. None of them seemed surprised.

Her friends cast pitying looks her direction.

Only Reverend Hammond and Genevieve appeared truly shocked.

"We'll fix this Penny," Genevieve stated, as if *fixing* what was obviously an ill-conceived match was easily done.

"We can send someone after him," Reverend Hammond offered.

"No!" Penny moved liked a wooden puppet as she handed Genevieve her bouquet and pulled off the veil, returning it to Birdie. "Here, I don't need this."

She refused to marry a man who had to be dragged before the preacher. She had more pride than that. But the town had that cursed deadline to meet and she knew they would hound her if she didn't get away.

Making a beeline for the door, she snatched her cape from a hook on the log wall and snagged a walking stick, which would come in handy in case she had to hike into the mountains to escape.

"I swear to you, Penny," Genevieve called out, "by day's end you shall be a bride."

God forbid!

Agreeing to a third marriage had been a mistake from the start.

Holding the walking stick upright, Penny burst through the door into the frigid morning air.

A cluster of miners standing outside parted as if she were Moses and they the Red Sea. Ignoring their curious stares, she headed up the street, being careful not to slip off the loose boards put down to function as sidewalks.

"Penny, slow down!" Birdie scampered up behind, holding her skirts so the hem wouldn't drag. "What a dreadful man. You're lucky not to be tied to him." She glanced over and did a double take. "Is that Grandpa Gus's walking stick?"

"Yes, of course. I grabbed it without thinking. I'm sorry."

"Oh, he won't mind if you use it. He swears he doesn't need it."

"But it belongs to him." Penny tried to hand over the walking stick. Birdie seemed reluctant to take it.

"Why don't you come inside where it's warm? I could make us some tea."

"No thank you."

"Coffee then."

Penny huffed as she quickened her pace. If her corset weren't laced so tight, she'd have run. "If you don't mind, I'd rather not talk right now."

Birdie finally accepted the walking stick. "Then come by later. Please."

"I will try." Penny kept her eyes trained ahead, quite unable to meet her friend's sympathetic gaze without bursting into tears.

She wouldn't be crying over Silas Powell. In a sense, his abandonment was a blessing. She'd started questioning their suitability on the first day she'd met him, although she had been determined to honor her promise, and had tried very hard to believe her intended was the person described in the letter.

Her fingers shook as she withdrew the folded paper from a pocket pinned to her jacket. Mr. Powell hadn't actually *written* the letter; Mr. Hardt had penned it on his behalf. Why had Silas's boss lied for him? She would give Mr. Hardt a piece of her mind, should she ever see him again. He had no business meddling in other people's affairs, even if he thought he was doing them a favor. She tore the letter into tiny pieces and tossed the bits into the air.

"*Chiquita*, wait!" Josefina nimbly leapt over a drunk sprawled across the sidewalk in front of the doctor's office. The exotic dancer never bumped into people or knocked things over. Penny envied her natural grace. "I have something for you that will help."

Was it another prayer card? The first one she'd given Penny hadn't worked.

Penny took the offering and glanced at one side, which showed the image of the infant Christ and his mother. The other side had a prayer in Spanish, which she didn't understand, having no knowledge of the language and being a strict Protestant from New England.

She didn't wish to hurt her friend's feelings, so she tucked the card into her cloak pocket. "Thank you, Fina, I'll keep it with me."

"Don't just keep it. Recite the prayer!"

Penny's breath clouded the air as she attempted to distance herself from the remaining, and more persistent, ladies in her wake. It was a miracle she had any friends left, considering her bad luck had been credited for everything from broken lamps to broken limbs.

"We'll send Sheriff Draven after that coyote to bring him back." Molly's shout came from close behind. A blur of gray and white crossed Penny's path, and she would've tripped and fallen on her face had Molly not caught her arm.

The goose honked as if it was Penny's fault.

"Better yet, Draven can skin him!" Molly's dark eyes flashed as she waved an imaginary knife. The sheriff, with his fierce scars and frontier sense of justice, *might* consider scalping as proper punishment.

Penny pulled her arm free and drew her cape closer. "I don't wish Mr. Powell ill." She dodged the honking gander darting around her skirts in a frantic effort to reach the person it believed to be its mama.

Molly swept the bird into her arms. "Daniel, behave yourself!"

What in the world would Molly do when she had a *real* baby?

"Mr. Powell jilted you! At the very least, he deserves to be horsewhipped."

"At least he had the good sense to leave town before I could kill him. My first two husbands weren't so fortunate."

Penny left Molly standing in front of the wagon repair shop wearing a puzzled expression. Perhaps the irony should've been explained, Penny hadn't actually *killed* anybody. Her first two husbands had died unexpectedly a short time after marrying her, so it stood to reason Silas might imagine he was bound for the same fate.

Upon reaching the place where the sidewalk ended—if two boards could be called a sidewalk— Penny stopped to catch her breath. She glanced behind her and sighed with relief. Her friends had stopped following. The men outside must've gone back into the saloon, but that didn't mean someone wouldn't try to find her.

Just over the bridge, a curving path led to the stables and corrals where the burros used at the mine were kept. As a child, whenever she'd been unhappy she had often fled to her family's barn for sanctuary.

Taking a deep breath, she started up the steep incline.

Her right side ached by the time she reached the split-log structure, where snow covered most of the bark-shingled roof. Thank goodness, someone had shoveled a path.

The stiff leather hinges resisted as she opened the door, but as soon as she stepped into the warmer interior she was greeted by the comfortingly familiar smells of hay and manure. A soft clucking sound came from somewhere in the back of the barn... Woody's hens.

Behind gated stalls, the donkeys raised their heads and regarded her with dark-eyed curiosity. Not pity or scorn. Animals were never judgmental. They didn't care if she carried bad luck like a disease. They wouldn't remind her that the town's future was at stake, or that everyone expected her to do her duty and marry before the deadline tomorrow.

Penny sank to her knees and allowed the pent-up tears to spill down her cheeks. Her chest ached and her heart felt bruised and battered. Oh Lord, she couldn't go through this again. Providence obviously did not intend for her to marry. How many disasters would it take before she got that through her hard head?

SOMETIME LATER, whistling drifted in from outside the partly opened door. Penny recognized the tune, *Buffalo Gals*, and also the whistler, Woody Burnside. He must be returning to his job. Not wanting to be caught crying, she hurriedly wiped her cheeks and came to her feet.

Woody stepped inside and then stopped abruptly, his eyes going round. "Hey there, Miss Penny. I didn't know you'd be coming up here."

Penny forced a smile. "I hope you don't mind. It's odd, I know."

"Not odd, just surprising." His gaze turned sympathetic. "You sure you don't want me to go after Mr. Powell?"

"Very sure." Penny brushed bits of straw off the satin skirt, her best gown. "I've come to see Shadow. I hope you don't mind."

"No, I don't mind." Woody picked up a pitchfork and went to work shoveling refuse out the manure door without questioning her strange request to pay a visit to a donkey. The townspeople considered him slow, but she had observed him numerous times and had decided he was just *different*…in a good way.

As Penny approached a stall, one of the smallest burros plodded over to greet her. She stroked the donkey's dark, velvety nose and rubbed between its furry ears.

Shadow nuzzled her hand.

"I'm sorry, I don't have anything for you to eat."

"Here you go." Woody offered her a handful of dried apples. "Stay as long as you like."

"Thank you. I'm most grateful."

He went back to work, picking up where he left off from his whistling.

Penny divided the dried fruit between the three burros, and petted them while they chewed contentedly. Being with the animals calmed her and helped her think more clearly.

In spite of the rough conditions, she liked Noelle and had enjoyed getting to know the townspeople and making new friends. She would be sad to leave, but her future obviously wasn't meant to be here.

Another woman could step in, one of Madame Bonheur's *girls* for instance. One of them—

Pearl—had married the sheriff. Finding husbands for the other soiled doves would be better for everyone concerned, save the madam. The awful woman would no doubt move back into her parlor house and resume her trade. Ever since she'd been kicked out so the incoming brides would have a comfortable place to stay, she mocked them every chance she got, and had offered them jobs *just in case*.

Penny's heart ached for the *unfortunate* women and others who were in desperate situations. She and Genevieve had talked often of how women needed to help each other. In fact, that was the goal of the Benevolent Society of Lost Lambs. She would write and ask Genevieve to recommend her for a position at the society to help *other* women make happy marriages. Surely, the matchmaker would understand and give her blessing.

A sense of calm came over Penny as she came to her decision. "Mr. Burnside, I'll be returning to Denver. I'd rent a rig, but I don't know the way back over the mountain to the next town where I can catch the train."

Woody stopped working, propped his arm on top of the pitchfork handle, and regarded her for a moment. He wasn't one to hurry a reply. "I sure am sorry you'll be leaving us, ma'am. Miezhen will miss you."

Penny touched an ivory comb tucked into her coiffure. Woody's Chinese wife had given her the unusual comb, shaped like a figure eight, as a wedding gift. The number eight, Meizhen had explained, was *good luck*. Sadly, the Chinese talisman hadn't been any luckier than the veil. Penny would return the precious keepsake if it weren't holding her hair in place.

"She has the other women, I won't be missed much."

"You're wrong there."

Woody might've meant what he said, but he was the one who had it wrong. After she left, the townspeople would breathe a collective sigh of relief, her friends included. She knew they walked on eggshells around her.

"Nevertheless, I've made my decision. My help is needed at the mission, where I can be of some good. If you would take me as far as the train depot. I'd pay you for your trouble."

Woody shook his head. "Ma'am, I can't make a decision like that without asking Mayor Hardt. We got to get his permission first."

Penny stiffened her spine. She needed no one's *permission* to decide what to do with her life, and certainly not the mayor's. In fact, he bore some responsibility for her present situation. His letter, rather the one he wrote on Silas's behalf, had convinced her to accept a disreputable scoundrel.

On the other hand, she couldn't dismiss Mr. Hardt's occasional acts of kindness. Besides offering his handkerchief that first day when she'd spilled Silas's whiskey, he had also came to her aid in the general store after she knocked over a display of canned beans. She ought to thank him, but she wasn't asking for his permission to leave.

Regardless, Woody did nothing without first consulting the mayor. She would be wasting her breath trying to talk him out of it.

"You needn't leave your work. I'll appeal directly to Mr. Hardt myself." According to Reverend Hammond, the mayor hadn't been too keen on the idea of bringing in brides to begin with, so she surmised he might be convinced to take her to the next town to catch a train.

"Thank you, ma'am. That would be best." Woody gripped the pitchfork. "Mr. Hardt, he'll be sorry you're leaving."

"Will he?" Penny found Woody's observation absurd, even amusing. Considering her presence had driven away one of the mine owner's supposedly *best workers*, Mr. Hardt should be glad to see her go.

CHAPTER 2

*C*harles Hardt, mayor of a struggling town and owner of the gold mine that had given it life, had run out of time. He might be bereft of luck, as well. Thankfully, he had food, so he returned to his cabin around noon to find something to eat.

He'd been at the mine since dawn, doing his usual safety checks and unloading the dynamite for blasting the new tunnel, all the while cursing himself for giving his crew a whole day off to celebrate the foreman's wedding. He should've limited the break to a few hours. That gold wouldn't find itself.

He had two days to prove that the town would prosper, or the Denver & Pacific Railroad wouldn't lay track through Noelle, and it would remain a struggling mining community. At worst, it would become a ghost town.

Muttering to himself—he had no one else to confide in—Charlie tugged off the thick leather gloves and shrugged out of his fur-lined coat, hanging it on a peg by the door along with his hat. He rubbed his arms to get the blood going and crossed to a squat iron stove. After adding wood, he poked at the embers with a fire iron until a blaze caught. It wouldn't take too long to warm the one-room cabin, and then he'd go back to the mine and freeze his ass off.

He opened a box labeled *Dynamite* and took out a loaf of bread wrapped in a kitchen towel, cut the last two slices, and layered in what was left of the smoked ham. Before he could take a bite, a knock sounded at the door. The taps were light, hesitant, as if the visitor wasn't sure of their welcome. Possibly it was one of the miners, though they generally forgot to knock at all.

"Come in," Charlie shouted, as he wrapped the sandwich in the towel and set it aside. When no one entered, he made his way to the unlatched door and jerked it open. "I said come in!"

A small, slender woman swathed in a black cloak took a quick step backwards onto the packed snow. She tipped her head back and blinked up at him from beneath a fur-lined hood. "Good day, Mr. Hardt."

Charlie's stomach did an odd flip. His foreman's bride...what was *she* doing here? "Good morning Mrs. Jackson, ah, I mean, Mrs. Powell."

A crease marred her smooth brow, and he wondered if he'd annoyed her somehow. All he'd said was *good morning*. Well, all right, so it was actually afternoon, but why would his losing track of time seem to bother her?

"May I come inside?"

"Be my guest." He walked backwards to give her room to pass and then peeked out to check, in case he'd missed someone. *Strange.* About now, she ought to be celebrating with her new husband, but Silas was nowhere in sight.

Charlie shut the door on the cold air.

"Thank you for agreeing to see me." She set a tapestry satchel on the floor. *Now why would she have a bag packed?*

After carefully drawing her hood off, she paused to secure an ivory comb holding her hair. She missed a few wayward strands, which curled down her neck.

He folded his hands behind his back so he wouldn't be tempted to help her tuck them back in place, or better yet, remove the comb entirely. "Did Silas send you up here?"

"No. Mr. Burnside suggested I speak with you."

"Woody?" That didn't make sense either. Woody should be at the barn...or maybe not. He might've gone into town for the wedding, but why would he send her up here?

"I hope I'm not interrupting." She cocked her head and looked at him questioningly, which shook him out of his musings. He was acting like he'd gotten hit on the head. She'd explain herself soon enough.

"Not at all. Here, let me take your cloak."

She undid the frog closure at her neck and allowed him to lift the heavy garment off her shoulders. He draped it over his arm, then glanced again at the closed door.

"Where is Mr. Powell?"

"On his way north, or west, I'm not sure. He didn't make an appearance at the wedding, and Mr. Burnside didn't say precisely where he went."

Her matter-of-fact tone, one she might use to comment on a spate of bad weather, threw Charlie into confusion. He couldn't have heard right.

"Are you saying Silas *deserted* you?"

She appeared to consider the question before answering. "The correct term is *jilted*. If we had said our vows and afterwards he left, that would be *desertion*."

Silas *had* stood her up. That didn't sound like something he'd do. Then again, Woody wouldn't have lied about him leaving, and Penny had no reason to make up this story.

Charlie shook his head. He'd missed the signs, like before, when he'd failed to recognize the fatal flaws in his partner's character, or for that matter, his wife's true nature. Only this time, the one who was suffering was an innocent woman.

His befuddlement dissolved in the heat of anger.

"That sorry son-of-a..." He clamped his jaw shut to stop the obscenity before it slipped out. And to think he wrote a letter of reference for the low-down skunk, and had gone so far as to say that Silas had *integrity*.

"You did right to come and tell me." Charlie's anger whipped into fury as he moved past her and hung up her cloak. "Wait here. I'll go after him."

Penny snagged his arm before he could retrieve his heavy coat. "No! I didn't come up here to ask you to find Silas and bring him back. I refuse to marry a man who doesn't want me."

How could any man *not* want her? She was lovely. Her eyes were a rare silvery gray, and she smelled faintly of apple blossoms, something he hadn't noticed before. Her skin appeared soft and smooth.

Lifting his hand, he stroked her cheek with the side of his thumb.

"Fool."

She blinked as if startled, then moved away from him with a look of alarm. Did she think *he* was the *fool*? She could be right. He wanted badly to keep touching her.

"You, um, have a speck on your cheek." Now he could add fibbing to the list of his sins. He ran his hand over the back of his neck in frustration.

Before the brides came to town, he had no need to worry about remembering proper manners. Curse Chase Hammond and his hair-brained scheme. This was his fault, too.

The flush beneath her cheeks heightened her skin's alabaster hue. Beneath the charcoal gray traveling suit, her waist was cinched in so small he could circle it with his hands. She was every inch a lady— from the top of her carefully coiffed curls to the bottom of her custom-made boots. Few well-bred women ventured this far west, and even fewer came to mining towns.

"I think we can agree that Silas is an idiot. Have you come up here to berate me for the part I played in this fiasco?"

"Do you mean by writing his letter? I did intend to give you a piece of my mind for meddling." Her finely arched brows puckered in a frown as she tugged the tip of each finger and removed her black kid gloves.

Perhaps she planned to slap him with the gloves? Wasn't as if he didn't deserve it. He hadn't thought of his favor to Silas as *meddling*, but he could see her point. "Mr. Powell is illiterate; he can't write or read. That's the only reason I agreed to help him."

Her lips parted in surprise, as if she'd just realized something. "So *you* read my reply?"

"Only because Silas couldn't." Charlie offered the half-truth. So what if he had anticipated reading her letter. He still recalled what she'd written: the heartbreak of losing two husbands, her desire for a fresh start, and the unexpected joy and optimism that his words had inspired. Her response had renewed his determination to save Noelle and make it better in order to give Penelope Jackson the kind of place she deserved.

Guilt lassoed his conscience, jerking him back to harsh reality. Regardless of his intentions, he'd misled her and had enabled an ill-fated betrothal. Now it was his responsibility to fix things...somehow.

"Did Mr. Powell happen to mention to Woody why he left?"

For the first time since she'd arrived, she

wouldn't look him in the eye. Instead, she dropped her gaze and her color deepened. "In so many words, I'm bad luck."

Bad luck Penny. Oh, he'd heard the gossip, blaming her whenever some mishap occurred and she happened to be around. But he would call down anyone he caught spreading the nasty rumors She wasn't responsible for random accidents. "That's balderdash."

"You don't believe it?"

"Do you?

Her dismayed expression made it clear she did believe it. Those superstitious idiots had wounded her tender heart. Reassuring her was the least he could do.

"There's not a thing wrong with you."

Her gaze turned reproachful. It was obvious she thought he was lying. He didn't appreciate having his word questioned. However, their conversation had drifted into an emotional realm where he was out of his depth, and he wasn't venturing any further. He preferred action to words anyway.

Charlie went to the table and pulled out the chair with the least wear and tear. "Here, have a seat." He wished he could offer her a comfortable cushion, but he didn't spend his gold on fripperies. "Tell me what brings you up here, if not to send me after the rascal, or horsewhip me for recommending him."

"Neither, I assure you." She didn't move from her position by the door. He assumed her hesitancy was due to his earlier impropriety. He'd mind his manners from now on.

"Are you hungry?" He fished in his pocket for his penknife in order to split the sandwich. Breaking bread seemed the quickest way to assure her she'd be cared for, in spite of the actions of an undeserving cur. "I'd offer you more, but I haven't been to town lately to buy groceries."

"Yes, I noticed you haven't been around."

Had she now? He liked hearing she'd taken notice of his absence because it meant she'd been looking for him. Not that it mattered one way or the other.

"Yeah, I do like to keep an eye on things. Lately though, I've been too busy up at the mine to come down and check on how the weddings are going." If he had been paying attention, he might've caught Silas on the way out of town and persuaded the low-down belly-crawler to behave like a gentleman.

Penny moved a few more steps into the room, like a cautious doe might approach a watering hole. She put her hand on the back of the chair he'd pulled out for her, and he waited for her to sit. When she didn't, he remained standing. "I hate to trouble you, except… I'm not sure I can count on anyone else."

Her confidence in him triggered something close to pleasure, only warmer. "Ma'am, I'm honored you'd seek me out, and I'd be pleased to offer my assistance."

"Excellent. I wish to leave as soon as possible and require an escort to take me to the Denver & Pacific Railroad depot."

"Leave! Why the heck do you want to do that?"

She retreated a few steps. He had to remember not to raise his voice and frighten her. But he couldn't allow her to just give up and skip town. Circling the table, he kept his tone low and friendly as he approached her. "Of course you're upset, who wouldn't be? But you can't just pack your saddlebags and ride off. What about your agreement?"

She jerked her chin up and her eyes flashed, reminding him of lightning inside a storm cloud. "I believe it was Mr. Powell who broke the contract. Therefore, I am freed from our agreement."

Charlie threaded his fingers through his hair, purely frustrated. Her timing couldn't be worse. "Free from the contract you made with Powell, yes, but Reverend Hammond wrangled the railroad into a meeting day after tomorrow. He's promised to bring twelve married couples as evidence the town is growing, not shrinking."

"*I* did not sign a contract with Reverend Hammond, nor did I sign anything with the railroad."

Her forceful declaration stopped that argument. Besides, he had no right to question her. True enough, she'd broken no promises. He, on the other hand, hadn't kept his commitment to find more gold and secure the town's future. Who should be held more accountable?

He conceded with a nod. "Sorry, ma'am, for questioning your honor. You aren't responsible for saving this town. I am."

Her chin lowered and the resolute glint in her eyes gave way to a softer, quizzical expression. "That wasn't my point, and I don't think anyone believes that you are solely responsible for the fate of the town."

"Pardon me for disagreeing, but I founded this town. My gold built it, and I aim to ensure that my gold will save it."

She looked around in frank disbelief. Given his bold statement, she might be thinking he should have more to show for himself than a one-room cabin with a few sticks of furniture. "Are you saying the mine isn't drying up?"

He folded his arms across his chest and repeated the answer he'd given to his crew, to the townsfolk... to anyone who doubted. "We'll strike a new vein soon."

Her gaze returned, questioning. "In two days?"

A muscle in his jaw jumped, and he clenched his teeth to stop the irritating tic. He couldn't guarantee he'd succeed in two days. Two months? Perhaps.

He still thought Chase Hammond's idea to order a passel of mail-order brides qualified as crazy. But the local land agent, who had personal ties to the railroad board, had vouched for it, and the weddings would buy the extra time needed to find more gold. Which meant he couldn't allow this bride to escape.

"Mrs. Jackson, please, stay and help me—I mean *us*—fight for Noelle. I'll bet there are dozens of men eager to wed you."

Her eyes grew bright with tears.

Oh no, not that! He wouldn't know what to do if she started weeping.

She blinked until the moisture vanished, and then a brittle smile appeared, which somehow hit him harder than her tears. "You haven't been in town much lately, so you may not have noticed, but the men cross to the other side of the street when they see me coming."

Just hearing about that kind of cruelty toward her

put him in a temper. "They'd better not when I'm around. I'll break their legs."

"Thank you, I think. Though that wouldn't change anything, other than keeping the doctor busier than he already is. Even Mrs. Walters is having trouble finding a suitable candidate for me, although at this point she believes any man might do. She wants to match me up with some big hairy trapper who wears bearskins and only comes to town every few weeks."

Charlie could think of only one white man who fit that description. "Do you mean Kinnison?"

"His name sounded Indian."

"The Utes call him *Kyi-yee*."

Penny shrugged. "Frankly, I don't care what they call him, I'm not interested."

Who could blame her? Zeke smelled like a bear, as well as looked like one. Sadly, he hadn't always been a recluse, but he would be the last person on earth to get roped into marriage.

Charlie rubbed his hand over the bristle on his face. He hadn't broken the record for fewest baths in a year, but it couldn't hurt to shave more often. But he wasn't volunteering to take Zeke's place. "Go back to town with me. I'll buy you something to eat at Nacho's, and we can discuss other options."

"I told you I'm not hungry, and I am *not* getting

married." She whirled away and grabbed her cloak. "If you won't help me, I'll find someone else."

Doubtful, considering the whole town knew what was at stake. Still, it was possible she'd find a way to accomplish her goal, or—*God forbid*—set out alone across eight miles of the wildest country imaginable. Regardless, he couldn't let her get away. He had a responsibility to the town, and to Penny. He'd gotten her into this mess by writing that letter, and he refused to allow her to slink off in shame and wrap herself in wounded spinsterhood for the rest of her life.

"Don't leave. Let me get a few things together and I'll bring around the wagon." He picked up his wrapped sandwich, located a few pieces of jerky, and stuffed everything into a flour sack. That ought to last until they circled back before nightfall.

He had roughly five hours to persuade her to stay. With the way things were going, that might pose a bigger challenge than convincing her to eat.

Who would marry her? He could think of several miners who'd jump at the chance to wed a beautiful lady, but he wouldn't recommend even one of them. He might be the only available man in town who had the social standing suited to Penny's genteel upbringing.

His heart started racing even though he was

standing still. What the heck was he *thinking?* He wasn't ready to marry again. He had enough responsibilities without adding a wife—no matter how lovely, or tempting she might be. Besides, she might leave him in the end anyway if he didn't meet her expectations, whatever those might be. No, *he* didn't have to marry her. Not if he could come up with a better option.

"Well?" Penny adjusted her hood. "Are you going to stand there all day, or will you take me over the mountain to the train station?"

CHAPTER 3

*T*he sun had risen over the treetops and its blinding rays reflected off the pristine snow in a patchwork over the mountainside. More snow covered distant ranges, and the breathtaking vista reminded Penny of a Christmas card.

Noelle hadn't been so idyllic twelve days ago when she and the other brides had arrived in the midst of a snowstorm. At least today it wasn't snowing. Yet. Blizzards were undoubtedly a frequent occurrence up here in the high altitudes, which was another good reason to retreat to a lower locale.

Penny shifted on the buckboard seat to adjust her cape. Riding in a wagon equipped with runners would make for easier travel along the winding roads that led to the closest town, where the railroad line currently ended. She resisted a tug of guilt on her heart. Someone else could save Noelle. She had tried to live up to her commitment, but Fate had other ideas.

While Mr. Hardt checked the traces, she tucked one of the thick blankets around her and burrowed her gloved hands into her lap. Somehow the cold managed to slip through the layers no matter how many she put on, and she appreciated the extra blankets her escort had provided. He didn't seem to mind the cold so much. His buckskin coat with its fur lining apparently kept him warm. Also, he'd been living up here for at least the past three years and would be more accustomed to the weather

The mayor was something of a mystery. The townspeople she'd asked didn't know, or wouldn't comment, about his past prior to founding Noelle, other than to say he'd come up from Texas a little more than three years ago and had shown up with a little more than a donkey and some mining gear.

Now, he owned the mine, as well as most of the buildings in town. Yet he lived in a sparsely furnished cabin that appeared only marginally nicer than his workers' homes. Everyone in town agreed he obsessed over gold. But whatever wealth he'd gained, he didn't put on display like the factory owners back east. He went about town dressed in the same type of denim jeans and durable shirts as the miners wore. But the way he carried himself, shoulders back and head up, bespoke confidence and pride. Regardless of his attire, he would instantly be recognized as someone *in charge*.

Earlier he'd claimed responsibility for ensuring the town's survival. Was it pride that explained such an arrogant point of view? Or was there more to it?

His lean form and long-limbed stride reminded her of the sleek mountain lions that prowled the wilderness not far from town. He even moved as stealthily as a big cat. Two days past, he'd come up behind her in the store and she hadn't heard him approaching until he'd spoken a greeting. Startled, she had knocked over a display of canned goods. He'd apologized for frightening her and insisted on picking them up. A moment ago, he scoffed at her remark about having bad luck. Maybe he thought she was simply clumsy rather than cursed.

He tromped back through the snow and climbed onto the seat.

Penny glanced away, not wanting him to catch her staring. Just a short time ago, she'd been prepared to marry Silas Powell, but she hadn't given her erstwhile groom another thought after arriving at the mayor's cabin.

"Ready?" Her escort's voice came out muffled

from behind the woolen scarf he'd wrapped around the lower half of his face. Only his eyes showed beneath the black hat brim, but she was struck by how very blue they were. She'd heard people call his gaze *cold*, but she disagreed. Those eyes heated her all the way down to her toes.

She nodded and adjusted her scarf to cover her nose.

He picked up the reins. Heavy leather gloves now concealed his hands, but she could recall, in exquisite detail, the sensation of those long, lean fingers curved beneath her chin and the soft stroke of his thumb on her cheek. His touch had released a charged current, which enlivened every nerve in her body. She could still feel a residual tingle.

The icy snow crunched, as the metal runners broke free. Then the sleigh lurched, throwing her backwards. Mr. Hardt snaked his arm around her before she tumbled back into the wagon bed. With a grateful sigh, she leaned against his side.

He tightened his embrace, making her realize what she'd done.

She jerked up straight and pulled her cloak tighter around her. My, but she was *much* warmer now. "Thank you. I really am ready this time."

Penny pretended not to hear his muffled chuckle. What he thought about her didn't matter. If the good weather held out, they would be at the train station before dark, where she would bid him farewell and never see him again.

As he guided the mules up a path, past the entrance to the mine, her gaze wandered back to his strong profile. When he glanced over, she looked away, mortified to be caught staring at him. For the next several hours, she would focus her attention on her surroundings, not the man sitting next to her.

Metal carts used to haul rock sat empty on a narrow track that went from the mine down to the stamp mill. The rhythmic pounding regularly heard throughout town came from heavy steam-powered stamps that pulverized the gold-rich quartz. Thus, the mine's nickname. But now *The Drum* was silent.

"The stamp mill isn't operating today?" she observed.

"The men have the day off on account of the wedding."

"But there wasn't a wedding."

"That doesn't mean they're not celebrating."

Penny peered down beyond a collection of rough canvas tents at the base of the mountain, further on, to the rough timber structures facing a snow-packed road.

The men were indeed celebrating—in the street. Fights were daily occurrences in a town where saloons outnumbered stores, and the most prosperous businesses appeared to be sporting houses. Filth, violence and disease were rampant among all the populations, both men and women, whether white, Chinese or Indian. Even upright leaders like the pastor and Dr. Deane couldn't seem to influence a change.

She cast an accusing glance at the man who carried a title implying authority. Did he even notice or care about the reality of his own town? "The letter you wrote for Mr. Powell described a very different place."

"Maybe I just see it differently."

Ah! So the opinions expressed had been his and not her erstwhile groom's.

"Noelle is a town of promise and possibilities," she quoted. She didn't need the letter to reference because she'd memorized it. "That's what you wrote, I remember. How do you look at *that* and see promise and possibilities?"

"I don't look down, I look up." He nodded in the direction of the mine. "We'll soon be hauling lots more gold out of that mountain. Then things will turn around."

Penny wished she had such certainty about her own future. "What makes you so sure you'll find what you seek?"

"Because I won't give up. By next Christmas, Noelle will have twice as many stores, paved roads, and I've promised Chase Hammond a brand new church."

She wasn't yet convinced the vision would become reality, but she admired Mr. Hardt's tenacity. In the letter, he'd conveyed in eloquent terms his aspirations for the little town, as well as his hopes for the future. Those were his sentiments. So it stood to reason, his personality had imbued the phrases that had fired her imagination and touched her heart. Mr. Powell hadn't lived up to her expectations, because she'd grown attached to the wrong man.

A sick feeling lodged in Penny's stomach. *No*, she couldn't harbor affections for Mr. Hardt. She hardly knew him. Besides, he'd never shown the slightest interest, except for that odd moment in the cabin.

"Look there at that long tom."

She turned her attention to where he indicated, at the frozen river running behind the town. The *long tom*, she supposed, was the structure of flat wooden troughs, built on a slant, following the river's course. At present, it looked in ill repair.

"That's where we sluiced our first thousand in gold. I started out panning in some of the lower rivers and streams until I found this place. It yielded enough for us to invest in supplies for hard-rock mining after I found evidence of more gold."

"Us?"

"Me and my partner."

"I didn't know you had a partner."

"Don't anymore. He made off with a fortune in *my* gold."

"Did you catch him?"

"Yep. Caught him red-handed. He was tried in a miner's court and sentenced to hang."

Horrified, she lifted her hand to her throat. She'd heard about the vigilante justice meted out in mining camps. Thieves were fortunate to be banished. "Sentenced to hang? For stealing?"

"If you take a man's gold and leave him without money for food or supplies, it's the same as killing him. Life out here is harsh."

Not a speck of pity.

"And unforgiving?" she chided.

"It can be."

For a man who penned such heartwarming prose, Charles Hardt sounded surprisingly cold-hearted. It was just as well she should open her eyes and see the truth. The sensitive man she'd imagined from reading his letters wasn't the one sitting next to her. That was a figment of her imagination, dreamed up out of loneliness.

"Forgive me if I think it strange, that the same person who would approve a death sentence for his friend would give a town a name like Noelle." Penny returned her attention to the scenery and tried to ignore her disappointment. Besides, her lofty expectations were irrelevant, considering that he wasn't the man she'd come to marry.

CHARLIE KEPT his attention trained on the road ahead, while mentally kicking himself for veering off-course, talking about his partner, rather than coming up with reasons for Penny to remain in Noelle. The whole story about what had happened with Robert Cortland was ugly and more complicated than he wanted to go into. But if he let stand her poor impression of Noelle's original inhabitants—him included—she definitely wouldn't stay.

"For the record, the sentence wasn't carried out. Somebody hauled my ex-partner out of the hole we'd put him in, and he got away."

There. Now they could drop this discussion about frontier justice.

"You did the right thing."

He threw a surprised glance her direction. "What makes you think I helped him?"

"He was your partner and at one time you must've been friends. I'm sure you couldn't bear to see your friend hang, even if he deserved it."

She'd misunderstood him. He hadn't helped Robert Cortland escape. Admittedly, he'd felt *slightly* relieved at not having to watch a man he'd once considered a friend hang. But that was beside the point. A short time later, he'd hired a ruthless bounty hunter to make certain no thieves would get away in the future. Wisdom advised keeping that detail to himself.

He guided the mules off the road and onto a trail, which led around the mountain. Hopefully, she wouldn't notice they were headed in a completely opposite direction from when she'd first come into town.

Penny threw a confused look over her shoulder. "Are you sure this is the right way?"

Apparently, she noticed.

"Are you worried I don't know where I'm going?"

"No. I suppose I'm simply confused."

Her apologetic response tweaked his conscience. He hadn't outright lied, and he wasn't acting out of self-interest. He was doing this for the good of the town.

To distract her, he took a turn a little too fast,

which caused Penny to slide in his direction. If need be, he could catch her.

She wrapped her arm around his and held on tight.

Charlie smiled at her instinctive reaction, which had been to reach for him. It felt good to be needed for something other than monetary gain. Olivia had only married him to get the ranch, and he'd been kidding himself to think otherwise. The women he'd been with since charged for their services.

How could any man *not* be drawn to Penny's spontaneous warmth and her compassionate, caring nature? This last unfortunate incident had shaken her faith in herself. Once she met someone who appreciated her, she would be a devoted partner. Her desire to escape could be more about her opposition to the town, rather than her reluctance to marry. She'd questioned how he could look down and see anything good in Noelle. Somehow, he had to get her to see the town the way he saw it.

"I named Noelle after my daughter."

Penny glanced over sharply, and above the scarf her eyes widened with surprise. "You have a daughter?"

Charlie took a deep breath. He'd misspoken and found this conversation was harder than he thought it would be. "She died five years ago, when she was three months old. She took a bad fever, and in just few a days she...she breathed her last breath in my arms."

He hadn't been able to come to grips with his child's death and had stayed stone cold drunk for months. If not for Chase Hammond, who'd taken an interest in him and helped him dry out, he might've put a bullet through his whiskey-saturated brain.

He needed to make peace with his friend. He'd been furious when Chase had picked a bride for him. Would he have been so angry if the preacher had selected Penny? Honestly, no.

"Now I understand what you meant when you said Noelle is a place of promise and possibilities," Penny said softly. "You were remembering how you felt about your child, and you feel the same way about the town."

Just like that, she grasped what he couldn't find words to express. She seemed so attuned, or maybe her insight didn't have a thing to do with him and she was just a woman with great sensitivity. Maybe that was why he felt safe unburdening his heart.

"Noelle was born on Christmas Eve. We'd run out of food and we were living in a tent. She was the only speck of joy in our lives. What a tiny little thing she was, with thick black hair, like her French Creole mother. She would've been a beauty." Charlie's voice grew rough. He'd forgotten how inconvenient and messy emotions could be, and how painful.

Penny didn't offer meaningless condolences. Instead, she moved her hand up and down his arm in a reassuring gesture. She'd written about her own devastating losses, and it infuriated him that ignorant men had piled on the suffering, blaming their fears on her *bad luck*. If he could convince her to stay, he would make sure no one went around spewing anymore of that poison.

They rode along in silence—the peaceful kind, like two old friends.

"Did you lose your wife to sickness as well?

The warmth in his chest shrank into a cold knot. He should've known this question was coming, and it was natural that she'd wonder. He could say, *yes, he lost her* and leave it at that. But it wouldn't be the full truth. Penny had given him nothing but the truth, even when it didn't show her in a very good light.

"The day after we buried Noelle, she left me."

Charlie kept his attention on the trail because he didn't want to see whatever might be on Penny's face. Pity, perhaps. More questions. She got quiet again so the direction of their conversation must've made her uncomfortable. Not as uncomfortable as he felt, he'd wager.

After another moment, she finally spoke. "She shouldn't have walked out. You didn't deserve that."

Odd, that she would defend him. "How do you know what I deserve?"

"I don't have to know. Whatever you did, or think you did, could be forgiven. That's what love does."

She spoke like she understood the elusive emotion.

Charlie glanced down at Penny's hold on his arm. Her touch warmed a cold place in the middle of his chest. Being kindhearted, she might want to offer comfort, but didn't know what to say. She didn't have to say anything. He was long past needing sympathy when it came to Olivia.

"I acknowledged my sins, and gave her what she asked for."

"Which was?"

"A divorce." And that was all he intended to say. He'd let the conversation get too personal. Revealing more wouldn't improve Penny's opinion about the future of Noelle.

She moved her hand up his arm again. Did she even realize what she was doing? "Whatever happened, it didn't stop you, and I can see how your suffering has made you more compassionate and generous. You've given people places to work and jobs to do. The doctor told me you paid for your workers' medical care after a mine accident last year then made the mine safer."

Her litany made him sound like a saint, which would be funny if it weren't so ridiculous. What would it gain him if his workers died and the town shriveled up? She lauded him for acting out of self-interest, which only proved she was a sweet, gentle woman. They could use more like her in Noelle.

"Why don't we dispense with formalities? Call me Charlie."

Her lips twitched, a small almost imperceptible reaction. "Not Charles?"

She even teased gently.

"That does sound more dignified, doesn't it? You reckon I ought to go by Charles?"

"Oh, no, don't. Charles sounds stuffy. I like Charlie much better."

The spontaneous smile she beamed at him caused his breath to get stuck halfway up his wind-pipe. He had to clear his throat before he could reply. "Glad to hear it."

He sincerely hoped she also meant she liked him, the person, not just his name.

"Do you mind if I call you Penny?" Her name suited her. The heavy tresses currently hidden beneath her hood had a shiny copper sheen like a newly minted one-cent piece.

"No, I don't mind." She murmured, and glanced away. She had to be blushing, even though he couldn't see the evidence beneath the scarf that concealed most of her face.

Pleased, Charlie shook the reins at the plodding mules. Penny wouldn't remain in Noelle if she disliked the man who presided as mayor, so gaining her good opinion made sense. They might even become friends, and that would be another reason for her to stay.

After a bit, her head began to bob. Later, her chin dropped to her chest. *Poor thing*, she had to be tuckered out, having probably not slept much the night before her wedding, and what had happened since was enough to tire anyone out.

"You can lean on me. Take a nap."

She jerked awake, tensed, but after a moment, relaxed against his shoulder. "Thank you, Charlie."

He smiled, and couldn't stop smiling. Everything was going according to plan. Eventually, this path would take them right back to where they'd started. When Penny realized where they were, he would say he'd been distracted and took a wrong turn, but they wouldn't be able to make it to the next town before nightfall. She might not be happy, but it would keep her in Noelle another day...and give him a chance to get her married off.

CHAPTER 4

$\mathcal{P}$enny slowly opened her eyes. She and Charlie had been chatting like old friends, but at some point she grew tired and must've drifted off. She lifted her head off his shoulder. Leaning on him wasn't proper, even if it did make her feel safe and warm.

"Oh good heavens!" She stared in horror at the sheer drop just beyond the other side of the wagon.

The wind, whipping at her cloak, sent a spray of white flakes whirling into a chasm.

Penny hugged Charlie's arm for reassurance, as well as to keep him from sliding off the seat and toppling to his death. "Where are we?"

"On a short-cut."

She craned her neck to look at the terrifying drop. "It looks unsafe."

"These mules are sure-footed. We've been this way many times." Charlie's nonchalance might be intended to comfort, but she knew better than to think it was genuine. He had to notice how treacherous the road had become; and it wasn't really a road, more like an old trail that wound around the side of the mountain.

Another gust swirled snow around them.

She held her hood with one hand, while keeping an arm firmly linked around Charlie's. "Do we need to be this close to the edge?"

He chuckled, as if what she'd said was meant to be funny. "Don't worry. I won't let anything bad happen to you." He turned his head and brushed his mouth against her hood.

Had he just given her a kiss? The possibility brought a smile to her face. *Oh good heavens.* He only meant to reassure her, and she would be grinning like a fool when the wind tipped the wagon and pitched them into eternity.

"We'll be off this road soon. A little ways up, the road bends and we'll hit a flatter stretch."

She squinted to find the bend he indicated. The wind kept the snow stirred up, making it hard to see far ahead.

As a distraction from her worries, she turned her attention to Charlie. When they'd started out, she'd half-expected him to be taciturn, certainly not talkative. Then he opened up and revealed things about himself that he admitted he didn't normally share. After hearing his heart-wrenching story, she felt even more connected to him, as if they'd been traveling in the same direction on different roads until their paths had finally crossed in Noelle.

Charlie slowed the mules, and the wagon slid to a stop.

Startled out of her daydream, Penny let go of his arm and sat up straight, which was what she should've done earlier instead of clinging to him. "What's wrong?"

When he hopped out of the wagon, her heart nearly stopped. Good Lord, he had to be inches away from the edge.

"Be careful!"

He looked up and his blue eyes gleamed with amusement. "I will. You sit tight. See that rock slide up ahead? I've got to clear a way to get through." After tying up the reins, he trudged through knee-deep snow to a mound of rocks that blocked their path.

Her gaze followed the rockslide up the mountain. She might not have noticed the opening, except for the reinforcement beams, one of which had collapsed when the rocks gave way. "That looks like the entrance to an old mine."

"It is. This is where we started three years ago, but then..." His voice trailed off as he rolled a boulder aside, and then another, and another. His labored breathing sent vaporous clouds into the cold air.

"Then?" she called out. "What happened?"

"We didn't find much gold. Lost a man when something went wrong." He tossed another rock over the edge. "I found a *floater* on the other side—a chunk of rusty-looking quartz that's broken off from a bigger vein—and we started digging where the mine is now.

"If this one is abandoned, what happened to cause the rockslide?"

Charlie looked up, squinting in the sunlight. "Not sure. Might've happened when we blasted through back then. Or it could be water freezing then melting that broke away the rock.

"Nothing could melt out here." She clenched her teeth to keep them from chattering. Sitting still, she would turn into an icicle. Moving around would keep her blood flowing, and she could help speed up the process of clearing the road.

She climbed down, careful not to shake the

wagon. The mules turned their heads to look at her as she passed. Nothing seemed to bother them. Not the narrow path, or the dizzying drop-off, or the freezing weather.

"What are you doing? I told you to stay in the wagon." Charlie heaved a cannonball-sized rock off the mountain. She cringed at the noise as the rock hurtled down. Although she supposed any sound was better than silence, which would indicate there was nothing over the edge, just vast emptiness.

She rubbed her arms. "I need to move, or I'll freeze."

He shook his head like he disapproved, but then he gestured to the rockslide. "Don't lift anything bigger than your fist."

"Do you believe me to be a weakling?" Penny bent and slipped her hands beneath a stone roughly the size of her head, and to prove a point she lifted it. *Oh dear*, it was heavier than she thought. But if she dropped it, that would just prove *his* point. "See? It's not that heavy."

Beneath the hat brim, Charlie's frown deepened. "Be careful."

After barking the warning, he went back to work.

Barely able to hold onto the rock, Penny shuffled toward the edge. Not too near, just close enough to toss it over. Having snowshoes would have made this much easier, but when they'd started on this journey, she hadn't thought she'd be walking around. She slid one foot forward and then the other.

The snow suddenly gave way. There was nothing beneath it.

Her heart slammed against her chest. With a terrified shriek, she let go of the rock and tried to step backwards, flailing her arms in a windmill motion, which instead of helping, sent her feet sliding forward, following the rock down the mountain.

CHARLIE DROPPED the rock he was holding and twisted around at the blood-curdling scream.

The back of Penny's hood vanished over the edge, and his heart stopped for a split second. Then he raced to where the snow had collapsed, taking her with it. "No, no, no," he chanted, and dropped to his knees.

The rockslide had torn away part of the road, and the snow must've drifted into a crevice, Penny hadn't noticed.

His insides knotted as he stretched out to look down.

Snow blanketed an avalanche of rocks that had tumbled down the slope. Perhaps fifteen feet below where he knelt, Penny lay sprawled on her back, having pin-wheeled through the drifts.

Charlie let out the painful breath he'd been holding. The rocks had halted her fall, which was good, but she was too still, like a porcelain doll a child had dropped.

"Penny? Can you hear me?" His voice came out hoarse, as if he'd been screaming for hours. "Penny?" he yelled louder.

She didn't open her eyes, didn't even flinch.

Dread squeezed his heart. "Penny! Wake up!"

Stop yelling and go get her. She hadn't fallen so far he couldn't reach her with rope. He scrambled backwards and got to his feet, forcing his mind to the task and not the sight of her lying there.

"She's *not* dead." He tried to pray as he ran to the wagon, but he ended up cursing. Where had God been when Penny ventured too near the edge? Forget God, where had *he* been? He should've been watching her. He shouldn't have let her pick up rocks. He had promised to *protect* her.

From a toolbox in the wagon bed, he retrieved a thick coil of rope, along with a pulley, which was used at the mine to lift heavy buckets. He guided the mules until the wagon was positioned as close to the edge as he dared, and then carried the largest rocks he could manage and heaved them into the back. There. Now the runners wouldn't slip and the wagon wouldn't tip over.

After hobbling the mules so they wouldn't be tempted to wander, he attached the pulley to one of the iron rods holding the runners in place. Once he got to Penny, he could pull her up and then haul himself up. Hopefully, she was just stunned, or maybe she'd hit her head and it knocked her out. She would be all right. She *had* to be all right.

Charlie held his fear in check as he let himself down the steep slope. The closer he came to her, the more worried he became. He moved carefully, so as not to dislodge the rocks beneath them, as he knelt and grasped her arm, then tugged her glove down so he could press his fingers to the inside of her wrist. He shook so hard he could barely keep his fingers over the delicate veins beneath her skin.

A pulse beat, steady and strong.

Pent-up fear rushed out in one great sigh. "Thank God."

Her lashes fluttered and she opened her eyes, staring at him with a vacant look that showed she had no idea where she was or how she'd gotten there. "Charlie?"

She knew him! She hadn't been knocked senseless. He wanted to scoop her into his arms and drag her against him, both laughing and weeping with relief. Without knowing how badly she was hurt, that would be foolish. He also didn't want to frighten her. She might not realize how far she'd fallen, or how precarious their position. If these rocks shifted, they could both tumble down the mountain.

"You gave me quite a scare." He tried to smile, but suspected it looked more like a grimace based on her alarmed expression. "Are you in pain?"

She winced as she propped herself up on her elbows. "A little."

"Don't get up." He caught her arm to prevent further movement. "Just tell me where you're hurt."

"What happened?" She looked around, and her confused expression shifted to stark terror. "Oh my God. I fell!"

He caught her as she jerked upwards and held her firmly against him so she wouldn't disturb the rocks. "Calm down, I've got you. You're safe. Just don't move around too much. Let me get this rope on you."

He hurriedly untied the rope from around his waist and secured it around her. "Here now, I'm going to pull you up. It'll be easy as pie."

She tightened her arms around his neck, squeezing so tight he could hardly breath.

"Good, your arms aren't broken," he rasped.

She loosened her choking grip and he sucked in air.

"I'm s-sorry." Her whole body trembled.

"Nothing to be sorry about, it'll be all right." He stroked her back, longing to soothe her fears. There would be time for that later, after they got to safe ground.

"Penny, honey. Let me go so I can pull you up. Soon as you're safe, untie the rope and throw it down to me. I'll come up and join you." He spoke in a calm, even voice, despite the palsy affecting his insides. If he showed fear, she might panic, and then they would be in big trouble.

PENNY HELD her breath until Charlie pulled himself up the side of the mountain. Then he was beside her, untying the rope she'd thrown down to him after he'd hoisted her to safety. By the time he tossed the rope and pulley into the workbox, she knew they would be all right, but she couldn't stop shivering.

Besides being miserably cold, she hurt like

someone had taken a stick and beat her all over. Still, thanks to Charlie she hadn't frozen and died on the side of that mountain.

"We have to get you somewhere warm." Charlie moved the larger rocks out of the wagon bed, pushed others aside and helped her up. He grabbed the blankets on the seat and wrapped them around her.

"Y-you need a b-blanket, too."

"My teeth aren't chattering." He crawled over her and onto the seat. "I can't turn around. We'll head for that bend. Hold on; I'll get you home."

Penny hugged the blankets around her, resting her head on one of the folded quilts and curling up in a ball, trying to stay warm. Each bump sent pain shooting through her bruised body. The cold went bone deep, and she was tired, so very tired. She struggled to keep her eyes open so she could tell him not to return her to Noelle.

"No...d-don't go b-back... The train station."

CHAPTER 5

*P*enny? Penny?

She could hear him calling, but she couldn't see him. Snow blew into a whirling maelstrom, blinding her. Oddly, the blizzard made everything black, not white. Her heart hammered in her chest as she groped in the darkness, seeking safety. "Charlie?"

Her foot sank in snow, the ground vanished and she fell, screaming.

"No!" Penny flailed in a blind panic as she fought to open her eyes. Someone caught her arms, but not before she struck them. She heard a pain-filled grunt. Whoever it was though, was strong and wrestled her onto her back, trapping her hands over her head. Large fingers laced with hers.

"Penny, wake up."

She wrenched her eyes open. As her vision adjusted to the dim light, she could make out Charlie's worried frown. She shifted, but didn't feel rocks beneath her, rather, a soft mattress. Why would Charlie be sleeping beside her? No, he wasn't beside her, he was half on top of her and pinning her hands.

She became achingly aware of his body...hard, long, and heavy. Worried, she tried to remember how she'd come to be underneath him, and—she glanced down at exposed skin—in just her underclothes. Licking her dry lips, she swallowed to moisten her mouth and tried to speak, but her voice came out breathless. "Wh-where am I?"

"Good. You're awake." His frown eased, as did his tight grip on her hands. "I brought you to my place and put you to bed. You were sound asleep when I carried you inside."

Ah, so *he* must've removed her jacket and skirt and most of her petticoats, and all the while she'd been senseless.

"Why did you undress me?" Her heart quivered. Did he intend to molest her?

"Your clothing was damp. I was about to go for the doc when you started screaming."

"How did I get wet?" Memories interspersed her wandering thoughts, and her breath caught. "Oh! I fell down the mountain in the snow, and *you* came after me."

"After I let you nearly get killed. Those rocks tore away part of the road, but the snow was piled up and it looked solid. I should've warned you. No, I shouldn't have taken you up there in the first place." His features grew strained, and he searched her face like he was looking for...she didn't know what.

"Forgive me."

She didn't agree that it was his fault. He couldn't have known the ground was gone beneath all that snow. But with him being so close, she was incapable of putting her thoughts into words.

She craned her neck and took notice of her surroundings: chinked log walls, a flannel blanket nailed up as a curtain over a window...which might explain why it seemed like nighttime, but not why he'd brought her to his—

She jerked her gaze to him, shocked. "This is *your* bed?"

"The only bed in the house." His lips twisted in a rueful smile, and he was so close she could see through the brown stubble covering the lower half of his face except for the area around a pale, thin scar marring his cheek. Up close, he looked dangerous.

Undressed, in bed with a man she didn't know well, she should've been terrified. Instead, she felt, while not exactly safe, protected. Other feelings he stirred, she didn't dare explore.

He shifted his weight, which only served to bring their bodies into closer contact. "How do you feel?"

"Sore, but alive." Oh yes, she was very much alive. The blood rushed through her veins like an unchecked flood. She curled her fingers, and he responded in kind, locking their hands together in an unspoken promise.

He won't let go. He'll keep me safe.

His valiant rescue would be proof enough, yet it wasn't the only reason for her certainty. Even before she fell, she knew she could trust him, and the knowledge gave her a sense of security she hadn't felt in so long.

He'd been looking into her eyes, but now he seemed to be staring at her mouth.

Oh yes. Please.

Had she asked aloud or only thought about kissing him?

Her heart thundered as he lowered his head. As he slanted his mouth over hers, her lips parted. She drew in the breath he exhaled.

Penny couldn't move, couldn't think! She could only *feel*...the lush pressure of his lips, his fingers flexing, holding her hands. His touch diffused a kind of healing warmth, which spread through every sore muscle, while pleasurable shivers raced across her skin. Fears fell away, her aches forgotten, as she lost herself in the kiss.

Unlacing their fingers, he moved his hands to her hair, threading his fingers through the loose strands and using his thumbs to stroke her face and trace her ears. He broke the kiss, only to forge a trail across her cheek to a surprisingly sensitive earlobe.

"Penny." Her name, whispered in his rough Texas drawl, sent another burst of shivers cascading over her skin. "So sweet."

She'd never known kissing could be so pleasurable. In her past marriages, sex had always been a perfunctory act. Charlie was teaching her differently. But he was giving, not taking, and in turn, it made her want to give him the same pleasure. Slipping her fingers beneath his suspenders, she traced the hard planes of his back.

He came back to her mouth and this time the kiss was more demanding, but she was ready and answered with her own demands. She wanted him with a fierceness that surprised and almost frightened her. Only a few hours ago, she'd been ready to commit to being a spinster, but that was before she knew how it felt to truly *ache* for someone.

"Do you have any idea how desirable you are?" he whispered against her neck.

No, she'd had no idea at all, not until he'd showed her.

She cradled his head as he kissed down to the scooped neck of her camisole.

"Beautiful," he murmured.

"Am I?" She wasn't aware she'd spoken the thought aloud until he lifted his head to look at her, disbelief etched on his features. Warmth flooded her cheeks. Oh, what he must think of her, begging for compliments.

"Lady, you are a vision." He emphasized his effusive praise with another scattering of kisses across her collarbone. "Let me show you." His whisper tickled her skin as he untied the ribbon closure.

She drew in a deep breath, which cleared her mind, at least enough to realize he intended to undress her and complete his lesson in passion. If she allowed it, he could soothe this deep hunger, a hunger she might never have discovered had he not brought her back his cabin to tend to her, just as he'd promised he would.

"We can't turn around, it'll take too long… Hold on. I'll get you home."

Something struck her that she hadn't realized before, having been too shaken to pick up on the unwitting clue he'd dropped. The road they'd taken that led up that treacherous path didn't go to the train depot. It circled the mountain.

She tightened her fingers in his hair. "The road you took, it led back here."

"What road?" he murmured.

The sly dog. He'd known all along where he was going. *Back home.*

"Charlie, stop," She tugged at his hair.

He didn't pause in his progress with unlacing her camisole, a kiss at a time, eliciting a quivering response. He'd misled her in the worst possible way, and now he took advantage of her weak state. Flushed desire heated into anger, and she gave a hard yank.

"Ow!" He lifted his head and regarded her with hooded eyes and a half-smile. "All right, darlin', I'll hurry. You don't have to—"

Furious, she drew back and delivered a hard slap.

He jerked upward with astonishment.

"Get off!" She pushed at his shoulders and arched her back, trying to unseat him.

"Easy now, calm down."

She wasn't an anxious mare that needed to be soothed before it was ridden. As he shifted to lift his weight, she gathered as much strength as her sore muscles could muster and shoved him, sending him off the bed.

At the hard *thud*, she winced. If he'd landed on his head, it was nothing more than he deserved.

Penny scrambled into a sitting position and with shaking hands began to retie her camisole. She couldn't believe she'd so easily fallen prey to this smooth-talking predator. "You...you *despicable* scoundrel!"

He popped up from the floor, his hair in wild disarray from *her* fingers plowing through it. Oh dear Lord, she had truly lost her wits.

He frowned at her. "What are you talking about? I didn't do anything you didn't allow."

She blushed hotter than a boiling teapot and snatched up the rumpled quilt to cover her exposed décolletage. "A *gentleman* wouldn't have attempted to seduce me and *lie* like you did."

"What did I lie about?" He propped his hands on his hips, where his shirt hung half out from her efforts to remove it.

She still longed to undress him, a realization that only fueled her shame. Her voice shook as she struggled to regain her calm. "Earlier you asked for my forgiveness, which at the time I didn't understand. But now it makes perfect sense. You told me you would take me to the train station, but then you took that road to bring me back to Noelle."

He threaded his fingers through his hair and released a heavy sigh. "I can explain."

"Don't bother. I won't believe a word you say."

His lips thinned into a tight line. Wisely, he made no further attempt to excuse his deplorable behavior. Instead, he ran his hand up his arm. A nervous gesture, perhaps? Or did it have something to do with that tear in his shirtsleeve? He might've hurt himself coming down that rockslide to rescue her.

Recalling the risk he'd taken to retrieve her dampened the flames of anger that burned against him. She felt a twinge of guilt for pushing him to the floor, though not near enough to apologize. *He* was the one who should be begging *her* pardon for being so underhanded. What hurt worse was how he'd pried open her heart, making her think he cared about her, convincing her she was special.

Tears stung her eyes. Embarrassed, she dashed them away with the back of her hand. "Why? Why did you do it?"

He looked to the door of the cabin, as if seeking an escape route, but then dropped his hands to his sides, his expression regretful. "For Noelle."

Noelle. The town he'd named after his beloved child. He would do anything for this mining camp that bore his daughter's name, even lie to a gullible woman.

Shattered illusions cut into her heart like shards of glass.

She glanced at the covered window. "What time is it?"

He retrieved his vest from a chair that he must've pulled up next to the bed to sit beside her. Even if he *had* treated her tenderly, she refused to feel a bit guilty for being angry about his deceit. He fished into the pocket, retrieving a fob and gold pocket timepiece. "By my watch, shortly after five."

"Far too late to make it to the train station, which of course was your plan all along. May I have my clothes?"

He put the watch away but made no move to retrieve her clothing. "Your traveling suit is damp." He gestured over his shoulder with his chin where she spotted a stovepipe. "I've put your things over by the stove to dry. There's no reason for you to leave tonight; you'll stay here and get some rest. We can work things out tomorrow."

"Stay here? So you can *ruin* me? No, thank you. I will *not* stay here." She jerked the quilt around her and slipped out of the bed. Her knees wobbled and her body remained bent. Good Lord, how would she walk out of here if she couldn't straighten up? Her muscles rebelled as she forced her shoulders back.

He moved to block her way. "I'll admit, I

shouldn't have taken advantage, but you're in no shape to go anywhere."

"Get out of my way."

"Hold on." He reached for her arm. When his fingers closed around a tender area, she winced. After he dropped his hand, she could see the dark, discolored flesh on her upper arm.

"Sweet Jesse," he said in a hushed voice. He curled his fingers lightly around her elbow and his worried gaze traveled her exposed arms and shoulders. "You're bruised."

This wasn't news to her. She could feel each and every one, and she wanted nothing more than to crawl back into bed—no, not *his* bed, not if she wanted to maintain any semblance of respectability. "I am well enough to dress and go back to town."

"Where will you go?" He sounded as if he cared.

Prior to her wedding, she'd been living at *La Maison des Chats*, a fancy house where the brides were put up after the sheriff had moved the fallen women across the street. Doubtless, the madam had moved back into her cathouse. Penny wouldn't go there now even if she could. "One of my friends will give me a place to stay for the night."

Charlie kept staring at the bruise on her arm. "You need to see the doctor."

"Then I will ask Cara if she'll allow me to stay

with her and Dr. Deane. Will you kindly move out of my way?"

He remained planted in front of her. "Will you hold on just a minute?"

"Why? So you can tell more lies?"

"No! So I can do a proper job—" he dropped to one knee and reached for her hand—"of asking you to marry me."

CHAPTER 6

"*M*arry you!*" Penny exclaimed.

Charlie tightened his grip on her hand when she tried to pull away. He had lied to her, nearly gotten her killed by his trick, and if that wasn't bad enough, had lost control and dang near seduced her. And he would've succeeded if she hadn't kicked him out of bed. Only a low-down rascal *wouldn't* offer marriage. For the sake of Noelle, he couldn't let her leave; and seeing as it was his fault she'd agreed to wed a rat, he owed her too much to shame her by foisting her off on another man. At this point, his choices had narrowed down to one.

"You heard right. Marry me."

"Let me go."

She wrested her hand away and used it to prop up the quilt. He wished she would let the covers drop and just go back to bed with him. Things were simpler there, much simpler than the emotions ricocheting around inside his chest.

"I'm leaving." She shuffled around him.

He really didn't want to do this—

Well, yes, he did. He grabbed the quilt, and she walked right out of it. When she squeaked in protest and reached for it, he gathered her against him, being careful not to touch the bruises marring her arms and shoulder.

She stiffened, but to his relief, didn't fight him. Maybe it hurt too much. His heart constricted at knowing he caused her pain, physical or otherwise. He should've apologized first, then proposed.

"Penny, I'm sorry I misled you. But you were being so hardheaded about leaving, I couldn't think of what else to do. I needed time to convince you to stay."

"You could've presented your argument on the way to the train station. You didn't have to trick me." She tilted her head to look at him with pain-filled eyes.

Worried, he loosened his hold around her, but then she swayed, and he had to grab her again to keep her upright. "Are you hurting?"

"Not enough to stay here with you."

Charlie heaved another regretful sigh. He'd messed up his first marriage, and things weren't getting off to a very good start on his second attempt. But he *would* make this work for the sake of Noelle, and also for Penny. Both deserved his best effort.

He secured the quilt around her before scooping her up. "Let's get you back to bed. I'll fetch the doc."

"No, please, not the doctor. I'm just bruised." She buried her face in his shoulder. "No one can know I've been sleeping in your bed or that you undressed me. If word gets out, they'll never let me work at the mission. They demand ladies of the highest caliber."

"You *are* a lady, Penny! There isn't any higher caliber than you. But you don't have to go back to the mission. You can stay here and do just as much good as my wife."

He put his knee on the mattress, and trying his best to be gentle, deposited her on the bed. "I know you're madder than a hornet right now, but stop and think for a minute. You told me you don't have any family in Denver. Here, you have friends. If you're determined to be a matchmaker, you can help the rest of these poor fellows find wives. We've got lots of *unfortunate* women, too. You won't lack for opportunities."

Unable to resist, he pressed a kiss on her soft, sweet-smelling hair. She felt so good in his arms, and kissing her had been pure heaven. Based on her passionate response the marriage bed would be no problem.

"Get away from me." She rolled onto her side and pulled the quilt up over her shoulder. "I'm only staying here because I'm too tired to explain this... this *debacle*," her voice wavered. "I'll be ruined."

"Not if you marry." He could offer to find her another husband, but knew he'd kill any man who tried to claim her. Besides, he'd gone too far to back down now. Not only that, but he was in a much better position to protect her. "If you're my wife, no one would dare speak ill of you."

She didn't answer.

He knew she was hurt and upset, but figured her outlook would improve after she had a good night's sleep. "Get some rest. We'll talk about it more in the morning."

"There's nothing to talk about," she replied in a dull voice. "If you're in need of a wife to make your quota for the railroad, you can marry one of the *sporting girls*. They would fare better with husbands, even with a man as despicable as you."

~

SOMETIME LATER, a creak woke Penny. It sounded as if a door had been moved, and she thought maybe Charlie had left to go check on the animals.

Shivering, she lifted her head and looked around. Not a glimmer of light shone from around the blanket hanging over the window. If that cloth was supposed to keep out the cold, it sure wasn't working very well.

She pulled the covers over her head.

Earlier, when he'd carried her back to bed, she'd considered defying him and leaving anyway, but her muscles wouldn't cooperate, and she only longed to sleep. Not to mention she wasn't up to explaining her predicament. Besides, she knew what everyone would say. They'd tell her: *marry the mayor; he'd acted out of desperation; his motives were pure; he was the town's most influential citizen and she ought to be thankful he'd offered for her.* That's what they would say—and she didn't want to hear it! She wasn't marrying Charlie; she wasn't marrying *anyone.*

She tried to ignore her body's needs, but ignoring the urge didn't make it go away.

With a sigh, she threw back the covers and slipped out of bed. Hopefully, her host would have a chamber pot nearby. She located what she sought under the bed—thank goodness she didn't have to go very far to find relief—and afterwards stood up and pulled the quilt around her.

Across the room, an orange glow shone from behind the grate on the wood stove. Her jacket, skirt and petticoats were draped over two straight-back chairs positioned in front of the only source of heat. If she could retrieve her clothing, she could be dressed and ready to go at the break of dawn.

Something soft brushed her ankle, and Penny sucked in a sharp breath as she jerked her foot up. *What was that?*

A long shadow darted across the floor away from her.

She screamed.

"Penny? You all right?" Charlie appeared near the stove. He must've come back inside and laid down, and some creature had slipped in behind him.

"Something got inside the cabin." Who knew where that *thing* had gone? It could be over near him, or even behind her again and had scooted under the bed.

Penny whirled around and leapt onto the bed, hugging the quilt and shuddering with revulsion. "I think it's a big rat!"

Charlie didn't act alarmed.

Maybe he wasn't afraid of rats?

He seemed far too unconcerned as he strolled

across the room and lifted a lantern from a hook near the door. After lighting it, he held it aloft. "Where did you see it?"

"It touched my leg, then it ran over there," she said, pointing to the opposite wall. "But it could be anywhere now, just keep looking!"

The light played across the floor and over the shelves mounted on every wall. *Could a rat get up there?* With all the clutter, it would have plenty of places to hide.

"Where are you," he murmured, as he walked around, holding the lantern out. His suspenders dangled down the sides of his trousers, and his shirt and hair were even more rumpled than before, when she'd had her hands all over him. The memory of her appalling lapse in judgment triggered a hot blush.

"Be careful; that rat might bite you," she warned him.

She thought she saw a quick smile flash across his face before he set the lantern on the table and bent down to scoop something off the floor.

"Come here, you. I should've left you in the barn." Charlie straightened, and her heart nearly stopped. In the crook of his arm he held a long, furry creature.

"What is that?"

"This is Bandit. He's a ferret."

Penny sat upright, still keeping the quilt pulled up to her chin. She'd read about ferrets but had never seen one up close, nor had she heard of anyone befriending one, much less naming it. "Aren't those rodents?"

"Now you've offended him," Charlie said dryly. "He *eats* rodents."

The ferret crawled up Charlie's shoulder and curled around his neck. Its eyes gleamed red in the lantern's light and had an accusatory glint as it stared at Penny.

"Don't look at me like that. I've never met a ferret before."

"Then it's high-time you did." Charlie walked calmly over and sat on the side of the bed, but she scooted away.

He took the ferret from around his neck and cradled it like a baby. "Penny, meet Bandit."

A mask across the ferret's face explained the name, along with the black markings on the tip of its tail and paws.

"I bought him off a trapper last year. He was a little thing then, but he's grown fast."

Bandit's forepaws had fierce-looking claws, although he didn't appear inclined to use them at the moment. In fact, the ferret seemed utterly content to rest in Charlie's arms.

Feeling braver, Penny shifted closer. "Is he friendly?"

"If he likes you he's friendly. I wouldn't call him tame, though."

"But you keep him for a pet?"

"Wouldn't say that, either." Charlie stroked a finger over the top of the ferret's head, which belied his denial that the animal was his pet. "I keep him around as a practical matter, because he's good at catching mice."

"You could've gotten a house cat," Penny pointed out.

"Didn't want one. Didn't want a ferret either, but he's not much trouble. He's got a burrow underneath the barn, sleeps most of the day and comes out at night. When I went to check on the mules, he crawled into my coat. I figured he might be cold, so I brought him inside. Sorry if he bothers you. He's just curious."

The ferret twisted its neck to look at her, his nose twitching, as if trying to determine what manner of creature she might be.

Penny ventured reaching out, and Bandit allowed her to stroke his head. She didn't want Charlie to think she disliked his pet after all; she'd only been startled. "I love animals, most of them anyway. I'm not fond of rats."

"He doesn't like rats either, but I've seen him go after them if he thinks he can make a meal out of one. An old Indian told me he prefers prairie dogs. Later in the spring, I plan to take him someplace he can be with his own kind and catch the food he likes best."

Penny's outrage with Charlie had cooled over the last few minutes. Even if she wasn't ready to forgive him just yet, his tenderness toward the small creature showed a side of him she hadn't seen before. He hadn't rescued the little ferret solely to have a mouser.

"Making a special trip to reunite Bandit with his own kind is admirable. You have a soft heart, Charlie."

He glanced up. "About some things I do."

Caught off guard, Penny blushed. She looked away, unable to meet his eyes for fear he'd see just how tender *her* heart had become. He'd slipped past her defenses again, with the help of his furry friend. "I should've known Bandit was complicit in your plan to wear me down."

The little creature slipped out of Charlie's arms and began to dig at the bed covers, as if it was trying to burrow. Penny lifted a side of the quilt and stroked the ferret's soft fur as it slithered underneath and curled up next to her.

She arched an eyebrow in accusation. "And he's just as determined to steal my covers."

Charlie gave her a half-smile that turned her insides to mush. "Bandit likes you, I can tell. He knows you won't hurt him, and he doesn't mean to hurt you."

"I suppose you didn't mean to hurt me either."

"No, I didn't, and I admit I made a mistake. Give me another chance, Penny."

Dratted man, he could melt her heart with just a look.

His accomplice slipped out from the beneath the covers and crawled into her lap. The ferret came up on its back legs and reached for her.

Was it trying to give her a hug?

"The two of you are incorrigible," she said with a smile, running her hand down the ferret's slender back.

Bandit pawed at her loose hair, and she drew back, startled. "Oh my! What are you doing?"

"Stop that." Charlie slipped his hand beneath Bandit's middle and brought the struggling ferret over to him. He started laughing as he plucked something out of its paws. "Why, you little thief."

Bandit wriggled until Charlie set him free. Then he hopped across the bed in an odd, frenetic dance, before jumping to the floor and vanishing.

Straight-faced, Charlie offered her a hairpin. "Got to watch out. He'll steal hairpins, jewelry...anything he thinks is a treasure."

"You named him well. Were you the one who taught him to steal?"

"Don't blame me. Thievery is in his nature."

"As being a charlatan is in yours?"

Something flashed in Charlie's eyes. Humor, yes, but also a flicker of regret. "Maybe somewhere south of righteous, though not as low as a snake oil peddler."

"You were peddling a falsehood." She was no longer teasing.

He grew serious as well. "I won't mislead you again or take advantage, you have my word on it. And if after tomorrow you still want to leave, I'll buy you a train ticket myself."

Penny's heart longed to forgive him, but her better judgment warned her to remain wary. He had nearly succeeded in seducing her with very little effort. On the other hand, she could use a little more time to heal before being jostled over mountain roads, and one more day would make no difference in the outcome. He had vowed to be on his best behavior.

"All right. One more day," she agreed, clasping

his hand. Just that one brief touch was enough to send a warm flush to her face.

His confident smile reappeared, and her heart beat ten times faster.

Oh dear! Had she just made a deal with the devil?

CHAPTER 7

JANUARY 5, 1876, NOELLE, COLORADO, THE
12TH DAY OF CHRISTMAS

*C*harlie rose early to put Bandit back inside the barn. He didn't trust the little thief not to get into things in the cabin, and he wanted to clear away any distractions from winning Penny over. He had to convince her to marry him by tonight in order to make the deadline.

He opened the door to the cabin, expecting to find her still in bed. Instead, he was greeted with the smell of coffee and the sight of Penny's bustled backside as she rummaged through the icebox. She'd changed back into the modest skirt and jacket she'd been wearing the day before. Looking at her now, no one would guess such a passionate woman was hidden underneath all that propriety—no one but him.

Smiling, he hung up his hat and coat. "You've already got the coffee going?"

She shut the icebox and spun around, then touched her pinned-up hair, acting self-conscious, although she smiled like she was glad to see him. "I found some coffee up there." She indicted the shelf next to the stove. "I hope you don't mind that I helped myself."

"Not at all. Were you looking for something specific, besides coffee?"

"Food."

"How about bacon and flapjacks to go along with the coffee? Does that tempt you?"

"I won't turn it down."

Would she turn down breakfast in bed?

Ha, she'd throw the coffee pot at his head. Food first, bed later. After the way she'd responded to him yesterday, he didn't doubt he'd get another chance, maybe even *before* they said their vows. She would be his wife by nightfall, he was sure, even if she didn't yet realize it.

He dug into a sack for the salted side of bacon, retrieved the frying pan and set himself to the task.

The idea of being a married man didn't bother him half as much today as it had yesterday. Their passionate—if interrupted—lovemaking, might have had something to do with it. He couldn't wait to pick up where they'd left off.

"What can I do to help?" she asked.

"You can whip up the flapjacks. Grab that apron hanging by the stove; there's flour in the bin, canned milk on the shelf, and bowls up there as well."

"A spoon for stirring?"

"In the dry sink."

"Bicarbonate soda?"

"Uh, try one of the shelves." He'd mounted shelves everywhere so he would have somewhere to put all the stuff that didn't go on the table or in the cabinet where he kept his weapons and ammunition.

She rattled around and after searching the nearest shelf, moved to the next one. "Charlie, you have a box of nails next to the canned milk...and why is there a pick ax hanging beside your coat?"

"I like to keep things off the floor."

"That's not the point. *Why* is the bicarbonate soda beside your shaving cup?"

He met her questioning gaze in the small mirror propped up behind the items she'd mentioned. "That doesn't make sense to you?"

"Does it to you?"

At that moment he couldn't recall why, but he was sure at one time it had made perfect sense. He shrugged and gave her a smile. She wasn't really scolding him as much as pointing out how much he needed a feminine influence. "I'll bet a woman like you could get this place organized in no time."

"An *army* of women, maybe." She placed the items she'd retrieved on the table and hummed while she mixed the batter.

He finished frying the bacon, feeling more content than he had in years. He enjoyed her tuneless humming, their banter, and the way she took over, as if she already lived there. "Is the batter ready?"

She brought the bowl over and set it on a cool stove cover. "Would you like for me to cook the flapjacks?"

"Let's work together. You pour, I'll flip."

"Agreed."

Penny dipped a tin cup into the batter, but when she reached over him to pour it into the frying pan, her elbow bumped the bowl. Charlie caught the bowl before it tipped over and moved it away from the edge.

She blushed seven shades of red, and got so flustered she dropped the cup into the bowl. "Oh my goodness!" she exclaimed, as she fished it out. "You might not want my help. With my bad luck, I may set the place on fire."

"You bumped a bowl, Penny. We all do it."

"Not as often as I do." Avoiding his eyes, she wiped her fingers on a rag hanging over the handle of the oven. He'd seen her bump into people and knock things over, yet she had a natural grace in how she moved. The problem wasn't simple clumsiness, but he wasn't convinced it was bad luck either.

"Maybe you need spectacles."

She darted a sideways glance in his direction. "Dr. Deane said the same thing."

"He might be right." Charlie lifted the pan so she could see it better.

Still red-faced, she dipped the cup into the batter and poured a dollop into the hot grease without any trouble. "There's nothing wrong with my eyes."

He gazed into the clear gray depths. "Nope, not a thing wrong. You have beautiful eyes; the color reminds me of galena."

"You think my eyes are..." she paused, then asked, "what's *galena*?"

"It's an ore, the natural form of lead, and often has silver mixed in."

Her eyes widened and now he could see silvery striations shot through the darker gray.

Unusual. Beautiful.

"Is it valuable?"

He suddenly realized he was still holding up the frying pan and set it back on the stove. "Yeah, I'd say your eyes are valuable."

"Not my eyes. Galena."

"Galena?" Oh yeah, he'd compared her eyes to a rock. He probably could've done better than that. "Depends. Can't be sure until it's tested, and it can be costly to extract all that rock if you're not sure there's much value."

Which reminded him...

He'd been hauling out and pulverizing tons of quartz for months that had yielded less and less gold. Again, he'd taken the tailings from the mine to the assayer to have them tested to see if he was missing something. He needed to talk to Hugh to learn if he'd found anything new.

Charlie turned two more flapjacks onto the plate she held up, waited as she poured more batter into the skillet. "After breakfast, I could show you inside the gold mine. If you're feeling up to it, that is."

She gave him a speculative look. "Mr. Powell told me he doesn't think there's more gold to be found, and the miners are worried they won't have jobs for much longer."

That kind of talk could spark a mass exodus. How many others would be influenced by the foreman's disloyalty?

"You and Silas sure talked an awful lot before he pulled heel."

"Apparently, we didn't talk enough. He gave no indication he planned to leave."

Her remarks stirred another troubling thought. Charlie didn't like the idea he might be partly at fault for her groom's defection, even though Silas had obviously only heard what he wanted to hear. "Powell took a cowardly way out, if he left because he feared for his job. I never once told him we'd be closing the mine. Just because we haven't hit the mother lode doesn't mean we won't. That's how mining goes; not every yield will have gold."

He refrained from further explanation, knowing from experience how futile it would be. The more he'd reassured Olivia he *would* strike it rich, the less inclined she'd been to believe him, and Penny had absolutely no reason to trust his word at this point.

Besides, the less they talked about gold the better. These days, it was a topic guaranteed to put him in a foul mood.

After he stacked the last flapjacks on the plate, she took it to the table, and he followed with the bacon. "Where do you keep the syrup?" she asked.

He snapped his fingers. "Forgot about that. I'm out." *What else might be good on flapjacks?* He scanned the junk piled up on the shelves. She might have a point about his organizational skills…or lack thereof. "I've got a stash of honey around here somewhere. Collected it last summer."

"Do you recall where you put it?" Penny went back to the shelves, then looked at him over her shoulder with wry amusement. "Over by the shaving cup? Or perhaps inside this tool box?"

"Very funny. Now I remember." He strode across the room and retrieved the jar from inside a locked cabinet where he kept his rifles, as he explained his logic. "I collected honey on the same day I went hunting, so it makes sense I'd put it here where I keep the firearms."

By the time he turned around, she'd already taken her seat at the table. Her lips twitched as if she found something funny, which he assumed had to do with his makes-sense-to-him-but-questionable-to-her logic.

She rested her wrists on the table, and he could see she was concealing something within her closed hands. Charlie put the honey jar next to the plate of flapjacks then asked, "Did you find something else in an odd place?"

She opened her fingers and a tiny, hand-carved drum, painted red, rested in her palms. She picked it up by a thin gold ribbon threaded through a metal loop. "I found this in the tool box. I believe it's a Christmas ornament."

In all the excitement over the last few days, he'd forgotten about the ongoing prank he'd been pulling on the couples getting married.

Charlie released a low laugh, as he sat down. "I agree this time. That is an odd place for me to have put it."

"Mr. Hardt, you are a sneak." Her smile broadened. Apparently, *this* underhanded trick amused her. "So, you're the one who's been leaving ornaments on the tree as a gift for the newlyweds. That's very sweet, Charlie."

Sweet? This might prove embarrassing if word got out, and it would definitely ruin the tough-as-nails reputation he had worked so hard to establish. On the other hand, she seemed awfully happy thinking he was a sentimental fool.

"It's ah"—he shrugged—"just a prank."

"A prank? How's that?"

"The first day they put the tree up, I thought—" He'd thought how stupid a bunch of grown men looked, falling all over themselves to doll up a saloon, and losing their dignity over a bunch of women. But he couldn't say as much without offending her, and that was the last thing he wanted to do. "Reverend Hammond commented on how bare it looked, so I just decided—"

Her eyes lit up. "That you would play Father Christmas!"

Father Christmas? Charlie wiped his hand over his face, knowing he would never live this down.

"Prank or not, I think your gifts show remarkable creativity. The couples are thrilled, and each ornament is so fitting. We enjoyed it and would all wonder what the next one would be."

The admiration in her gaze just might make the embarrassment worth it.

"You like them?"

"Charlie, everyone *loves* them."

Did they? Why that should put him in a good mood, he couldn't imagine. Well, maybe he *had* enjoyed putting ornaments on the tree, then waiting for the couples to discover them, watching their faces as they mused about who might be leaving the gifts. He wouldn't go so far as to say he'd intended it to be *touching*; and this was just the kind of sentimental drivel that he'd wanted to avoid. He definitely wouldn't be putting the drum on the tree. How obvious would that be, considering his mining operation was called *The Drum*?

"Let's, um, keep this between us."

Disappointment clouded her features. "Very well.

If you insist on remaining anonymous, I will respect your wishes."

That was easy.

Now he was ready to dig into the meal they'd prepared together. The day hadn't started out half bad.

But Penny still examined the tiny drum with her forefinger. "This is exquisite. All the ornaments you've left on the tree are lovely. Where did you find them?"

Did they have to keep talking about this? He'd lose his appetite.

"I ordered a set of twelve ornaments out of a catalog some time back." He reached across the table and plucked the little drum out of her hands so she would stop obsessing over it.

Her expression softened to something approaching sympathy, only kinder. "You bought them for your daughter, didn't you?"

Ah, she was too quick, and far too smart. He didn't like how she could so easily read him. Not only that, but she seemed determined to flush out details he'd rather keep to himself. But if he evaded her questions, she would consider it more evidence of his deceitful nature. The best option seemed to be keeping her busy with something other than talking.

"Yes." He lifted the plate of flapjacks and offered them to her. "Now, can we eat?"

～

AFTER BREAKFAST, Penny helped clear the plates and cleaned up the dishes at the sink, using water Charlie had heated on the stove. After she had confronted him with her delightful discovery, he hadn't said more than a few words. She was half-sorry she'd brought up the tender subject, because it had ended their playful banter. Though it might be just as well. Learning more about his soft spots wasn't making it any easier to resist him.

She reached to place a dried plate on the shelf just as he turned. She bumped into him and the plate fell from her hand, but Charlie caught it before it shattered on the floor. "Oh goodness! You really ought to keep me away from anything that might break."

He waggled the plate. "Nonsense, we make a good team. You throw it and I catch it."

His good-natured teasing eased what could've been another awkward moment, and she found she could laugh about it because he didn't act annoyed. Or worse, scared.

"You have good reflexes," she pointed out.

"Maybe you should take up juggling."

His lake-blue eyes sparkled with amusement as he picked up the second clean plate and tossed it upwards. Catching it, he sent the other plate airborne and snagged that one, too.

"Shall *I* try?" She reached for one of the plates.

He pulled it back before putting both plates on the shelf. "Mm, I only have two. Maybe there's something else we can do together that doesn't involve breakables."

"Such as?"

"How about this?" He circled his hands around her waist and drew her to him.

Kissing him seemed the most natural response in the world. The touch of his lips reignited the fire he'd started the night before, and Penny wrapped her arms around his neck. *Oh yes!*

This was something they did very well together, and it didn't involve anything that could be broken.

Except for her heart.

Instantly, the fire fizzled, and Penny put her hands on his chest and pulled away. Charlie's actions could be excused; men always took sexual liberties when a woman made it so easy for them. But why was *she* allowing it, and not even feeling a bit ashamed?

She shook her head sadly. "What are we doing,

Charlie?"

His lips curled into a wicked smile and he tightened his hold around her waist. "If you have to ask, I must not be doing it right. Here, let's try again."

She kept her hands planted against his chest to keep him at bay. *Charming rogue.* He knew just how to tempt her, with his teasing smile and sizzling sensuality. "This is what I feared might happen. I should go back to town."

His smile faded. "You promised me one day."

So she had. But how would she hold out against his determined seduction when she possessed so little restraint? "You said you would show me the mine," she prodded, knowing that was as good an excuse as any to avoid another toe-curling kiss.

Charlie heaved a sigh—reluctance if she ever heard it—and finally released her. "I did say that, didn't I? We'll need light." He moved to one of the shelves and began to shift cups and jars around. "Wonder where I put those lucifers?"

Penny waited patiently until it became clear he wouldn't find them in the disorganized mess. *Now where would he have put a box of matches?*

She walked straight to the rough-hewn cabinet where he earlier found the honey and pulled open a drawer. "Ah, here they are!"

His mouth dropped open. "How did you figure

out they'd be in there?"

"Well, you said you went hunting, so I assume you took matches to start a fire, then put them in here when you returned your gun."

He grinned as he pulled on his coat and tucked the matches into his pocket. "Now you're thinking like me."

"I *know* how you think. That's different than thinking *like* you."

"If you say so."

He assisted her with her cloak and handed her the thick woolen scarf, which she wrapped around her neck and face before pulling up her hood and putting on her gloves. After they were bundled up, he opened the door and a frigid wind whisked inside, making her shiver.

He hesitated. "Are you feeling well enough for a walk?"

"I was feeling well enough to let you kiss me, so walking shouldn't be a problem."

After he showed her the mine, she would insist he take her back to town where they would be around other people. Except, she knew if they showed up in town together it would create even more problems. She would go back alone and deal with the inevitable questions.

Charlie stopped where he'd left the wagon

beneath a covered area protected by a low-slung roof. He rummaged through a toolbox in the back and then pulled out something, which looked like an iron spike twisted to form a candlestick. He retrieved another item from the wagon bed and offered it to her. "Have a keepsake."

"A rock?" She smiled behind her scarf as she cupped the *gift* in her gloved palm.

"Not just any rock; its galena. It's even got silver in it."

"Really?" She peered over the side of the wagon, and saw even more rocks. They hadn't been there when they'd started out on their journey, and she wondered when he'd collected them, and why? Did he think they were valuable? "Why did you put all these rocks in here?"

"The wagon had needed more weight to keep it in place when I attached the pulley to pull you up, and since we had an abundance of rocks up there, I put them to good use. I had a lot more, but I pushed all the bigger ones out."

"Oh. I thought... Never mind." Penny tucked the fist-sized rock into the deep pocket in her cape. Maybe it wasn't worth much, but she would treasure it anyway, just because he gave it to her. Though she wouldn't tell him that, of course.

He offered his arm, and after a short hesitation,

Penny looped her own arm through his and allowed him to escort her along a winding path, which led to the mine entrance.

As they approached, she saw the carts remained idle again today, and heard no noise coming from the stamp mill below, and wondered at the lack of obvious activity.

"Did you give the men two days off?"

"Two days? They're lucky to have one. They're inside the mine, I suspect, getting ready to blast that new tunnel, which is why we won't be staying long."

The wind gusted against her, as if to hold her back from the mine, and she hugged her cloak to prevent it from whipping around her. "I can't believe they're working in this weather."

Charlie put his arm around her and drew her to his side, so that his body blocked the wind as they walked. "You're starting to sound like Silas. He complained constantly about the cold."

"It *is* cold, Charlie."

"Yeah, I know, but the railroad isn't extending that deadline, and if we don't find more gold, they'll bypass Noelle...no matter how many men get married. We can't afford to sit out the winter. It's a matter of survival."

She gazed up at him, noting the determination etched on his face. He couldn't be very comfortable out here either, but from what she'd heard, Charlie spent every day up at the mine, working alongside his crew. "I very much admire your persistence, and even more so because you're doing this for Noelle and the people who depend on the town for their livelihood."

The widening of his eyes conveyed his surprise. "Is that a compliment I hear? I'm surprised you found something about me admirable."

She elbowed him for mocking her. "I believe I told you yesterday, I find many things about you admirable."

"Good. I couldn't ask for a better gift than to be in your good favor."

Coming from someone else, that might've sounded like empty flattery. But she knew Charlie meant it. He'd already shown he took into consideration her thoughts and her feelings...and even her pleasure.

Being this close to him heightened her awareness of the physical pull between them. Around Charlie, she felt more alive, yet also more vulnerable. He'd awakened something elemental and primitive, a force she'd never known, which must've lain dormant within her. The thought of losing control scared her to death. If she gave into her longings, what would happen?

She could fall in love with a man who didn't love her in return, *that's* what could happen!

This time it wasn't the cold making her tremble.

"You're slowing down. Are you tired? Here, I'll carry you."

"Good heavens, no." She stopped him as he tucked the odd candlestick under his arm, apparently intending to scoop her up. Fear gripped her and she backed away.

His expression softened. "Don't be afraid."

"I'm *not* afraid." But oh yes she was. She was terrified of her own weakness, which had gotten her into trouble before, and would again, if she continued to stay with him for the remainder of the day. Even one more hour would be too long. "I've been distracting you from your work," she insisted.

"What? You asked me to show you the mine." Confusion flickered across his face, and then his brows gathered. "You can't leave now, not after you gave me your word."

Breathing hard, she took another step backwards. "Only because you pressed me. I see no reason for us to spend more time together."

"No reason? I can think of a good reason." He had her in his arms before she could gasp. Pulling her against him, he covered her mouth with a fierce, demanding kiss.

CHAPTER 8

*C*harlie's frustration dissolved the instant Penny's lips softened beneath his, and she began kissing him in return, like she intended to steal his soul. He would gladly offer it up; it wasn't doing him a bit of good anyway. He fitted her body tighter against his, finding it much easier to show her without words a very good reason for them to remain together.

She tore her mouth away. "No! This is wrong." Planting her hands on his chest, she pushed, but this time he was ready, and didn't budge.

"It isn't wrong, and you aren't getting away," he whispered and drew back her hood so he could kiss her ear.

"Let go!" Her heel came down hard on his foot, surprising him with the pain.

"Dang it!" He hopped on one leg, but before he could grab her again, she whirled away, her cloak flapping as if she'd sprouted wings as she fled down the path leading into town. For a woman who'd fallen off a mountain only yesterday, she appeared very spry today, or else her eagerness to get away from him had overcome any lingering discomfort.

Charlie flexed the toes on his aching foot. He'd done exactly what he said he wouldn't do and had pushed her too fast. Still, he couldn't be implicated as the sole transgressor; Penny had returned the kiss, quite passionately...until he'd crossed the line. If she found the thought of marrying him so distasteful, he'd damn well let her go. She wasn't the only one reluctant to wed again, and there had to be an easier way to get a railroad.

As he limped on and was passing the stamp mill, he spotted the land agent stooped over at the side door, and hesitated in disbelief when he saw Percy messing with the lock. Charlie could think of no reason the railroad agent would need to be inside the building. Forgetting the pain in his foot, Charlie walked silently over to stand behind the other man. "Is there something you need, Penworthy?"

Percy whirled around, looking surprised...and a

bit guilty. "Ah, no. I was just seeing if you'd returned. Rumor has it you escorted one of our mail-order brides back to the depot. Frankly, I'm surprised that *you*, of all people, would break the deal we had."

Charlie's already touchy mood soured further. "I don't break deals."

"Yes, well, we agreed to twelve marriages, and I'm not sure Kinnison's will count since he isn't living inside the town limits."

"*Zeke* Kinnison got married?"

"Late last night to the matchmaker."

What a stroke of luck.

"There's no reason his marriage shouldn't count. He does pick up his mail in Noelle."

Percy sniffed and pulled a hankie out of his pocket. "That only makes eleven. What about the twelfth couple?" Percy's brow furrowed. "And don't expect us to accept another one of those prostitutes as a last-minute substitute. Draven and Pearl don't exactly fit the description of *respectable* couples."

"The deal was twelve marriages. Don't try to back out now; you're the one who championed this idea!"

"I'm not backing out. I'm just making the requirements clear, one of which is *you* have to come up with another bride and marry her."

"Me? Since when did this deal depend on *me* tying the knot? You just made that up."

"No, it was part of the original agreement, and I would know, considering I'm the one who drew up the document."

"Document? I don't remember signing anything. *Chase, the double-crosser, had ordered him a bride. Fortunately, the preacher married that one, and those two were a better match anyway.* "Besides, Chase married Felicity."

"He isn't the mayor." Percy straightened the round spectacles. "If you don't think you can come up with a bride, my uncle's offer is still good. Should you accept his bid, I'm sure he'll waive the requirement for you to marry."

Ah. *Now* it made sense, and why Percy had been so eager to get behind this particular bandwagon. He probably thought it was the cleverest scheme he'd ever cooked up; force a man who had forsworn marriage to get married, or sell out.

But even marriage would be preferable to giving the railroad control over the mine and the town.

Charlie's lips stretched into a smile. He'd go find Penny and talk some sense into her, but if that failed, he'd had no choice but to carry her back up to the cabin where they would finish what they *both* had started.

"Give your uncle my regards, and invite him to the wedding tonight."

Percy's scrunched his face in puzzlement. *"What wedding?"*

"Mine."

≈

"MORNIN' pretty Penny." Old Gus tugged the brim of his low cap and got to his feet.

When Penny had arrived at Peregrines' Post and Freight, the owner's grandfather was seated at his usual spot on the left behind the postal counter. She'd hoped she might find Birdie at her place on the right in front of the shelves where her fabrics were neatly stacked.

Birdie would know all about what was going on in town, but Grandpa Gus? Not so much. However, it appeared from a quick look around the empty office the elderly Mr. Peregrine had been left in charge—unless his grandson Jack was in the back working in his carpentry shop.

"Good morning, Mr. Peregrine."

"Call me Gus, or Grandpa Gus. We ain't strangers." Gus gave the counter an enthusiastic slap, which made Penny's nerves jump. "How's married life treatin' you?"

Oh heavens, his memory. Birdie would've told him what happened.

"Thank you for asking, but I'm not married." Had she stayed with Charlie, she didn't doubt she *would* be married, probably before the sun had set, which was why she had to leave. For his sake, as well as hers. Given her run of bad luck, the mine would dry up entirely the day after she spoke her vows.

"Ah, you'll be needin' yer mail." Gus started checking slots stuffed with letters and papers.

"No sir, I don't have any mail." *Who would write?* Her family was gone, and her closest friends were all here in Noelle.

"I'm looking for Birdie. Jack's wife." The older man might need reminding.

"She went..." Gus's scrunched his face into even more wrinkles as he stroked a long rust-colored beard. "Now...where did she go?"

"Never mind, I can ask someone else."

"No wait! I remember now; she's gone to deliver a dress."

"That's very kind. She's so talented." Penny wished she had half the skills Birdie possessed. She stopped to admire a day dress in burgundy velvet trimmed with matching lace. Beautiful, but not practical for where she'd be going to work. Plain gray wool would be more fitting.

"Miss Aggie has a beau," Gus informed her. He winked as if he'd just let out a secret.

Poor Agatha's troubles were certainly no secret, not after her suitor had publicly rejected her. But to Penny's knowledge, no one else had stepped up to ask for the elderly widow's hand. Apparently Gus hadn't heard, or else he'd forgotten.

Penny tried for a tactful, but true, response. "I believe her groom requested a different bride."

Gus gave a dismissive wave. "Aw, she didn't want him anyway. She's got somebody new."

"Really? Who?" she asked, humoring him.

The older man's golden eyes gleamed. "Guess."

Agatha's advanced years alone would preclude most offers, considering the local male population had an average age of less than thirty. None of the men were close to Agatha's age, except for— Penny gasped. "Oh, my goodness! *You?*"

"She's the reason I've been falling asleep with my head on the postal counter. It was all those late night meetings with my Aggie. We been seein' each other on the sly," he said with a teasing smile. Then he slapped the counter again. "Don't tell anybody!"

This news was certainly timely.

"All right. I won't tell, but you'd best not wait too long to ask for Aggie's hand. The town needs two more couples to marry, and she might get away from you!"

Gus chuckled. "That gal does move fast. But she says she's not in a hurry to make up her mind."

What on earth was she waiting for?

Penny sighed. The older couple might not tie the knot in time.

"Say, how're you getting along with yer new husband?"

Oh no, not again.

She gave him a gentle smile, determined to handle his befuddlement with kindness. "Thank you for asking, but I don't have a husband. Mr. Powell left town; maybe you hadn't heard."

"No, I heard. I'm talkin' about Mr. Hardt. Woody told me you and him went off together to the train station. Since you came back, I thought you must be married."

Penny blushed to the roots of her hair. She shouldn't have assumed Grandpa Gus had lost his marbles. He'd drawn the obvious conclusion, considering the facts. Everyone else would assume the same thing when she waltzed back into town, especially after she'd been gone all night and half the day. How was she going to explain her way out of this one?

"Mr. Hardt did offer me a ride to the train station, but a situation arose, and we had to return." She hated covering up for him, but to reveal the whole truth would result in certain ruin and compel them to marry, even if nothing had actually happened between them. "He's very busy up there at the mine."

Gus left his seat and came around the counter; his walking stick remained propped in the corner. Apparently, Birdie had been right. He didn't need it. He went over to the shelves where Birdie's fabrics were displayed, apparently searching for something. *Maybe his mind had wandered again.*

But then he began to speak. "I always did think you and Charlie Hardt were a better fit. He needs a tenderhearted, loyal woman, and you need a man who'll treat you with kindness, and who'll be generous with his praise and appreciate you."

Penny was shaken to the core. She had underestimated the older man's insightfulness.

"Mr. Hardt has been very kind," Penny acknowledged. In fact, recalling how he'd praised her body made her slightly breathless. Though he might not particularly *appreciate* her at the moment. "But he has no desire to marry." He'd only offered her marriage for the purpose of meeting a deadline, after all.

For her part, she had already pledged her loyalty to three men previously, and look where that had gotten her. Two were dead and one had fled. She had no reason to believe things would get better if she gave her heart to a man who didn't really want it in the first place. There had to be some other way to help him save the town.

"Ah, here it is!" The older man pulled something down from the shelf and brought it around to her. "I knew it was up there somewhere." He offered her a folded square of lace, which she recognized as the veil Birdie had made for her. The same one she'd given back. Her name had been written on a piece of paper and pinned to the fabric.

Penny touched the delicate lace, but then gently pushed his hand away. "Tell Birdie I very much appreciate her thoughtfulness, but I don't think I'll be needing a veil."

Gus shrugged and put it back where he found it. He pulled a stool up to a table strewn with leather fragments and picked up his awl. "Well, if you don't need anything, I'll get back to work."

Penny turned away, her mood even lower than when she'd arrived. "Goodbye, sir."

"Watch yer footing on the way out. Jack fixed the porch step, but life is still slippery for the stubborn."

THE PORCH STEP in front of the freight office might be less slippery, but the wide boards placed between buildings weren't so Penny watched her footing as she stepped to the next board. The planks had been put down for the convenience of walkers who needed to get from one place to the next without stepping in the filthy slush made from churned up snow, manure, and hot ashes thrown into the street to keep it from icing over.

Why had Grandpa Gus called her stubborn? She was simply being practical, wanting to find a way to help Charlie without committing both of them to an unwanted marriage.

"Look out!" A man grabbed her arms an instant before she walked right into him.

"Oh my! I'm so sorry!" She quickly backed up.

Hugh Montgomery swept off his hat and made a bow. "Forgive me, Mrs. Jackson, for not paying attention."

"No, Mr. Montgomery, *I* wasn't watching where I was going." Penny adjusted her hood, which had fallen back in the mishap. "I beg *your* pardon."

"Then under the circumstances I shall accept only half the blame." He followed his apology with a smile. The venerable English lord tried very hard to fit in with the other men in the mining community. But no matter what he did, he still stood out like a polished gem among uncut stones.

Speaking of uncut stones…

"I have something here I would appreciate your opinion on." Penny reached into her cloak pocket. Charlie had told her rock wasn't valuable, but it wouldn't hurt to ask the assayer to confirm it. Besides, as it had been a gift, she wanted to learn more about it. "Mr. Hardt said *galena* often contains traces of silver."

"Yes, that's true." Mr. Montgomery took the rock and turned it in his hands. His gaze flickered over her briefly before he returned his attention to the chunk of lead. "Did *he* provide this, along with the explanation?"

A nice way of asking if she'd been with Charlie. The town wasn't that big, and gossip spread faster than an epidemic. There was only one way to treat it, outside of a hasty marriage, and that was to admit to nothing and exhibit irreproachable behavior.

"We came upon a rockslide impeding the road near the other mine." She chose not to explain why she'd been with Charlie, or the exact details about what had happened. "Mr. Hardt collected some of the rocks. That's one of them, and I'm curious about its make up."

The assayer examined the galena with a thoughtful frown. "The other mine?"

"The old one, on the other side of the mountain."

Mr. Montgomery's eyebrows lifted as if the news

came as a surprise. "Did Mr. Hardt happen to accompany you to town? I have some information he might be interested in."

"No, he stayed behind."

The Englishman's enigmatic expression didn't give away his thoughts, but Penny could guess. What a mess, and one that could've been avoided if only Charlie hadn't deceived her.

"I do still plan to leave town. Early tomorrow, at the latest."

"Ah, then I'll see what I can do about testing this right away."

"Thank you, I'd appreciate it." She cast a quick look over her shoulder. *Was that Genevieve on the way to the Fulton's store?* The matchmaker would have some ideas for speeding up a wedding between Aggie and Gus—or would know what other options existed, if any. "Oh, I see Mrs. Walters, and I need to speak with her. You'll pardon me if I hurry to catch her?"

"Of course." Mr. Montgomery bowed, still holding the rock she'd given him.

"Give my best to Minnie."

"Certainly."

Penny hurried away, but her steps slowed as she drew closer to the store. She'd left without speaking to her friend, and even thought leaving a letter behind had been easier, it had also been cowardly.

Genevieve might be angry, at the very least hurt, and rightfully so.

Nervous of her friend's reaction, Penny anxiously peered through the window of the shop, but she sighed with relief when Genevieve saw her and her face lit up. The other woman waved and then rushed outside, and to Penny's further surprise, embraced her.

Penny hugged her friend. "Oh Genevieve! I imagine you're very cross with me. Will you forgive me for sneaking away?"

"My dear, I'm not cross, I am *relieved*. You have no idea how much I've worried." Genevieve drew back, her hands still on Penny's arms, her face damp with tears. "It is *I* who should apologize for pushing you into something you weren't ready to accept."

"You are more gracious that I deserve. I'm so glad you understand."

"Well, you made a convincing argument, and your advice to look into my heart was exactly what I needed to hear to make me realize that—" Genevieve, always so full of confidence, cast her eyes aside, seeming uncertain. "I do have some news…"

"Matchmaker! Thief!"

Penny turned with Genevieve to see who was shouting.

A disheveled woman staggered across the street,

her silken skirts dragging in the dirty snow. She clutched a bottle in one hand and shook her other fist at them. "A pox on both of you!"

"Good heavens, that's Madame Bonheur!" Rather, Betsey Smith, which was her real name. Penny hadn't recognized her at first, as the madam of the town's most popular fancy house didn't generally wander around looking like a common strumpet.

Her cloak hung open and her gown's plunging neckline was positively scandalous, even for a loose woman. Her ebony hair, always perfectly coiffed, hung in disarray, as if the pins had come out and she wasn't aware, or didn't care. Gone was the fake French accent, as well as any attempt at decency.

"Ignore her. Maybe she'll leave," Penny whispered. The last thing she needed was to be drawn into a public argument with the town's notorious madam.

The drunken wretch threw the empty bottle and stumbled this way and that, weaving across the road, barely missing being struck by a passing wagon. The few people on the sidewalks had started to take notice.

"You *ruined* my business!" the madam yelled. "Boum Boum ran off with that despicable miner, Angelique and Jolie packed their bags last night after the wedding and moved on. Jolie said if *you* could catch 'the bear,' they could snag husbands too. Bah! They're *whores!*"

Penny latched onto one particular word. She inquired in a side comment to Genevieve: "What *wedding* is she talking about?"

"Mine."

"You're *married?*" Penny gaped in astonishment.

A faint blush stained Genevieve's cheeks and an uncertain smile hovered. "I hope you don't think I— That is to say, I realized I knew him and I... Well, that's the news I wanted to share. I wed Mr. Kinnison last night."

Kinnison? Hadn't Charlie mentioned his name?

"The hairy trapper?"

"He's not so hairy." Genevieve's blush deepened. She put her arm around Penny's shoulders. "Let's go inside where it's warm and we can talk."

"Don't you turn away!" the madam yelled. By some miracle, she'd made it all the way across the street without being run down. "You ain't no better than me, just more expensive."

"I've had enough of this." Genevieve whirled around and stepped off the boards into the street. The anger flashing in her friend's eyes alarmed Penny. Genevieve needed to be careful; the mean-spirited madam was far too unpredictable, and it was bad enough that they'd drawn everyone's attention.

Even the shopkeeper's wife and the madam's daughter, Avis Fulton, came out of the store, perhaps having heard Betsey's obscenities. The young woman had traveled out here to locate her mother, and *this* was what she'd found—a remorseless harlot. Her sad expression was enough to break Penny's heart.

Genevieve faced off with her sneering tormenter. "You, Miss Smith, are inebriated. I suggest you go back to your room and sleep it off."

"Go *diddle* yourself." The whore's face twisted with hatred as she turned on Penny. "Wasn't enough your friend here sank her claws into the trapper, but you ran Silas off, then went after the Mayor. Yer stealing my best customers!"

Appalled, Penny could only shake her head.

"Now see here, you uncouth woman…" Genevieve straightened to her full height, which was still a few inches shorter than the madam, although Penny was about the same size. Right now, the woman's bloodshot gaze was trained on Genevieve, and there was murder in her eyes.

"Uncouth? I'll show you uncouth." The drunken woman rammed her hand down her ample cleavage and pulled out a small pistol.

"Betsey *don't!*" Avis yelled. "Look out, she's armed!"

Penny's instincts took over and she batted the gun, which went spiraling into the air. At the same time, Genevieve shoved the madam backwards.

With a furious howl, Betsey lunged forward and grabbed Penny's hair, yanking hard, which in turn caused Penny to fall against the drunken harlot, and down they went into the cold, dirty snow.

Sprawled on top of the madam, anchored by her hair, Penny struggled to free herself. The pain of having her hair pulled was nothing compared to the humiliation of being dragged into a public wrestling match with a whore.

CHAPTER 9

*A*s Charlie rounded the corner to the main road through town, he began to hear shouts and jeers. A crowd had gathered in front of Fulton's store, which meant a fight had broken out— nothing new— and everyone had gathered to watch, which was even less surprising.

"Let me go!" A woman's cry grabbed his attention. *That sounded like Penny.*

He took off running toward the mob. Who dared to lay a hand on her? "Get out of my way!" Men who didn't move fast enough got heaved aside.

Charlie jerked to a halt. *What the devil?*

Two women grappled in the dirty snow. The town's madam hung onto a hank of Penny's hair like a determined bitch with a bone, at the same time heating the air with a stream of curses. Penny hollered and pulled at the other woman's hair, while walloping her with one fist. Even though it looked as though Penny was holding her own, this wasn't a situation she was likely to find herself in.

The matchmaker and Mrs. Fulton had waded into the fray. They had a hold of the madam's arm, but every time they yanked, the motion pulled at Penny's hair. At this point, it was questionable who was helping whom.

"I'm takin' wagers," one of the mule drivers told him.

"Put your money on the lady," Charlie replied. He was tempted to let said lady pound the whore into the dirt, but for Penny's sake it was time to intervene.

The other women stepped aside as he strode over.

"That's enough." He grabbed the madam's free arm and jerked her to her feet. Once she let go of Penny, she tried to scratch him, but he was quicker and locked his fingers around her wrist.

The sheriff ambled over with three other ladies trailing behind, all of them talking at once in a frantic babble.

"Take this one." Charlie pushed the drunken whore toward the sheriff, who caught hold of her before she went face first into the slush. Wouldn't make much difference, she already looked like she'd been wallowing with pigs, and had a well-deserved bloody nose.

"Here, let me help you." He offered Penny his hand, and when she grabbed hold and he brought her to her feet. She was breathing heavily, her hair had come down, she had a smear of dirt on her cheek and muck down her skirts, and her cloak had gotten wet.

He tightened his grip, drawing her closer so he could brush back her hair to get a look at a row of scratches on her neck. That had to hurt. "If it's any consolation, your opponent looks worse."

Penny glared at the madam, whose arms were being held in Draven's tight grip.

"What're *you* lookin' at?" the whore snarled. She touched her face and then stared at her bloodied fingers. "She *broke* my nose!"

"An improvement, believe me," Charlie drawled, earning another blast of curses.

"That wicked woman tried to shoot us!" The matchmaker, who also had a fair amount of mud on her skirts, marched over to the sheriff and held out a small pistol, which Draven took and pocketed.

"Let's go, Betsey. You need to cool off." The sheriff hauled the madam in the direction of the jail.

"Show's over folks. Break it up," he called over his shoulder.

One man in the crowd whooped. The one Charlie had urged to put his money on Penny. "Come on, pay up boys!"

Penny stunned expression shifted to one of horror. She seemed at a loss as to what to do, and when she took a step in the deep slush she nearly lost her balance.

Charlie didn't hesitate to grab her, and he scooped her up into his arms. "I've got you."

"What are you doing? Put me down!" She smacked him on the chest.

"Here now, the fight's over. I'm on your side."

"You're embarrassing me." She dipped her head as if she didn't want anyone to notice her, though it was a little late to be acting like a wallflower.

The matchmaker moved in front of him and put her chin up, reminding him of a bantam hen. "Mr. Hardt, you are creating a scene and causing Penny distress."

He wasn't about to turn Penny loose, not now that he'd caught her. "I appreciate your concern, ma'am, but I'm taking Mrs. Jackson somewhere warm, where I intend to have a private word with her."

He shifted to get a better hold, and Penny

wrapped her arm around his neck. At least she'd stopped fighting him.

"It's all right, Genevieve. Arguing with him is a waste of time, believe me."

The matchmaker gave him a look, which told him she was taking his measure. "Have a care for her reputation, Mr. Hardt."

"You can depend on it."

Penny's reputation wouldn't be a problem for long. He figured she ought to be ready to marry him by now, if for no other reason than to put an end to wagging tongues.

PENNY'S TEETH rattled like loose rocks in a tumbler. In the midst of the latest humiliating episode, she'd suddenly taken a chill. Then Charlie had decided to play the part of Galahad. *What more could go wrong?* She'd sent Genevieve away because she couldn't bear to look her friend in the eye.

Granted, the madam had vexed her beyond what any sane person could bear. But the punch she'd landed had given her pure satisfaction. She had truly stood up for herself, perhaps for the first time in her life. On the other hand, she hadn't been standing.

As Charlie set off, she peeked up from where

she'd buried her head in his shoulder. It appeared he was headed for the saloon. *That wouldn't do. No, wouldn't do at all.*

"Where are you going?"

"You need to get warmed up before you take ill."

"If I can change clothes, I'll get warm."

"The bag with your clothes is still at my cabin. I'll borrow a wagon and take you up there."

An enticing image popped into Penny's head: being in his bed, wrapped in his arms. "No!"

"Then stop fussing and trust me." He kicked open the door to the saloon and carried her inside.

The assorted miners and ranchers who stood at the bar turned and stared at them; this wasn't surprising. She was a woman, and a scandalous one at that.

"You fellas clear out while I get Mrs. Jackson something to help her warm up."

At his order, the men moved away from the bar and filed out the door, all the while continuing to cast curious glances over their shoulders. Finally, the only other person left in the saloon was the barkeep, who turned his back to them and started cleaning the back counter, whistling softly.

Oh, why had Charlie brought her in *here*, of all places!

"I can't imagine what they're thinking," she murmured.

"They're wishing they'd put their money on you."

Betting on her, like they would a cockfight.

She dropped her head onto his shoulder. "I need some strong, hot coffee."

"Best thing for a chill is a shot of whiskey."

"No, thank you. I rarely drink more than a sip of wine."

Besides, who needed whiskey when she had Charlie's arms to warm her? Sadly, it was past time to pretend that she could remain hidden in a safe cocoon.

"Put me down, please." She tried not to sound too reluctant.

He carefully lowered her into a chair at the table closest to the potbellied stove. After feeding it more wood, the fire inside began to crackle. "Sit tight. I'll get you that drink."

Seeing as it was pointless to debate him, Penny unhooked her damp cloak so the warmth could penetrate her clothing faster. She scooted closer to the stove and leaned forward, relishing the heat on her face, and removed her ruined gloves so she could also feel it on her hands.

As soon as she warmed up, she would tell him

she intended to leave town. What choice did she have? Her luck hadn't improved. If anything, she'd made her lot worse. If she'd fleetingly entertained any thoughts of staying, she had just ruined it. He might even *want* her to leave. The thought put a knot in her stomach.

Charlie handed her a glass. "Sip this."

Maybe it would help, as he claimed.

She took a drink, and grimaced. *Firewater*, the Indians had aptly named it. Awful stuff. But Charlie was right about how quickly it warmed her insides.

He pulled a chair up next to her and sat. He'd gotten himself a glass, too, except he didn't drink it, and instead, withdrew a handkerchief and dipped it into his glass, then leaned closer and cupped his hand around the back of her neck. His palm diffused more warmth than the whiskey. When he dabbed the damp cloth over the marks on her neck, she sucked in a sharp breath.

"Ow! That stings!"

Charlie's frown conveyed regret. "Need to clean these scratches so they don't fester. Betsey's got claws...but you have a better right hook."

Penny closed her eyes as heat overtook her face. After he finished cleaning the scratches, she took a few more sips of her whiskey. It seemed not to burn so much as it went down this time.

He leaned back and set the cloth on the table. The tenderness in his expression put a lump in her throat. "So what happened?"

Penny sighed and shook her head. "I was talking to Genevieve. She's married!"

"So I heard."

"Yes, well, she was telling me about Mr. Kinnison, and that woman accosted us. *Madame* was very inebriated and we had words, then she pulled out a gun. When I knocked it out of her hand, she grabbed my hair and somehow we ended up on the ground."

Charlie rubbed his hand over his mouth.

"Are you laughing at me?"

"No, I'm not laughing."

"Yes, you are." She hadn't yet reached the point where she found the incident amusing, and wasn't sure she ever would.

Something the madam had said still niggled at the back of her mind. She didn't really want to know the answer, but the irritating question wouldn't go away until she'd resolved the matter. "She accused me of stealing her customers—you, for one."

Charlie's humor faded fast. "I can't lie and say I've never been there, but I'm not a customer; more like a landlord. Though considering her behavior today, I won't be renting to her again."

Penny didn't feel the satisfaction she thought she would. "I wonder where she'll go?"

"Are you concerned?"

"I hate to think of any woman being homeless and without a means of support, however distasteful."

He sat back in his chair and his mouth quirked in a half-smile. "Lady, you have a merciful heart. I admire you for that. It'll serve you well in a town with lots of sinners."

Penny finished the remainder of the whiskey in her glass. She *had* to tell him she was leaving. Tomorrow. "Charlie, I need—"

"What?" He leaned forward, and his blue gaze intensified. "Tell me what you need. If it's in my power, I'll give it to you."

"May I have another whiskey?"

CHAPTER 10

*O*f all the things Penny might've asked for, whiskey wouldn't have been Charlie's first guess, but he took her glass and returned to the barkeeper. Maybe plying her with liquor wasn't such a bad idea. It might calm her down. "Half a shot for the lady."

Seamus arched a bushy eyebrow as he poured a splash of whiskey. "Should I keep the boys outside a while longer?"

Charlie glanced at Penny. She'd been shaken by this latest incident, and it might not be the most ideal place, but he had to get her consent now and tie the knot as soon as possible. They were already here, so he could send for the preacher immediately after she said *yes*. Given how she'd responded to his kisses, it shouldn't be too difficult to get past her objections.

"Give me a few more minutes, then you can open the door."

Seamus winked. "You got it, boss. Good luck."

Charlie took the whiskey back to the table and sat down. He had a strong hunch Penny would turn him down flat if he again blurted out that he intended to marry her. He had to think of a way to get past her fears, which seemed mostly to be rooted in superstition. Assuring her he didn't believe in bad luck hadn't worked, so maybe it was time to try a different tactic.

He reached under his collar and took a leather cord from around his neck. When he held it out, the pendant flashed in the light. "I had that made from the first gold we mined here on this mountain."

Although it held a special meaning to him, it didn't hold any kind of power, other than what the wearer believed it did, but he hoped that would be enough.

Penny took the gift and studied it, rubbing her thumb over the lump of gold. "It's still warm from your skin."

His skin was getting warmer watching her rub that thing and imagining her wearing nothing but the necklace. Distracting thought, to say the least. "Wear it for me. For good luck."

Her eyebrows shot upward in a look of pure panic, and she thrust the necklace back at him. "No, I can't take your good luck."

He closed her fingers around the gold nugget. "You won't be *taking* it. I'm sharing it. Why are you always so certain bad things will happen?"

She gazed down at his gift with a pained expression. "Because bad things always *do* happen. When I was thirteen I came down with a fever, then my brothers took ill. I recovered, they didn't. My parents died less than two months later. Even my aunt was afraid to take me in, and made me stay in the servants' quarters, but she passed away too, right before the Colonel offered for my hand. He was older than me by some twenty years, but he was still hale and hearty—at least he was until our wedding night. I didn't marry again for another five years, and my second husband was a younger man who owned a successful factory. *He* said he was lucky too." She looked up and her eyes were dark with despair. "He died in a fire."

Fate hadn't been kind was all Charlie could think, but he refused to believe she was cursed, although telling her that wouldn't change her mind. Somehow, he had to rouse her stubborn nature and redirect it against the real enemy—her lack of confidence.

"I agree you've had a bad run. So what've you done about it?"

"Done?" She searched his gaze with a look of desperation. "I've prayed."

"And?"

"God hasn't taken it away."

"The Almighty can be unpredictable. I pray too. I figure God wouldn't have much use for me if I didn't make an effort."

"What are you saying? That I'm not trying hard enough?" An annoyed frown replaced the despair. *Good.* She needed to get her back up and fight. Not give up.

"I'm saying you should look at the positive things that have happened, and let that reassure you. Just over the past twenty-four hours, you fell off a mountain and lived to tell the tale; and you've won over a very discriminating ferret."

Her lips twitched.

"And we found out we make a good team, especially when it comes to cooking pancakes." He reached for her hands. "And kisses," he said in a low voice. Now was his chance to make his case for marriage. "Take a chance, Penny. Marry me."

The door to the saloon banged open and a cold wind swirled inside.

Penny looked past him, blinking with surprise.

Charlie shot to his feet and turned around, clenching his hands and itching to take apart the idiot who'd interrupted them.

Percy yanked off his hat. "Excuse me. Have I interrupted something?"

"You have. State your business, then leave."

"I just thought you might like to know your crew left town." Percy turned the hat brim in his hands. "Maybe now isn't a good time."

Charlie narrowed his eyes. "Is this some kind of joke?"

"No, no joke. A little while after the, er, altercation…" Percy's gaze darted past Charlie's shoulder at Penny and then back. "A representative from Folly's Peak came up to the miners standing around outside and told them he was looking for men to work a big gold strike. As soon as they heard about it, they left."

"You're lying. Those men wouldn't leave without telling me. They're loyal."

"Yes, well, I suppose you thought Silas was loyal too."

Seamus came around the bar, his brow creased with worry. "Are *all* the miners gone, then?"

Percy rubbed his chin as he thought. "The ones outside who heard the news are. I suppose a few of the men might've stayed, but I wouldn't know for certain."

The land agent dipped his head in a little bow. "Good afternoon, Mrs. Jackson. I'm glad to see you've returned. I hope you'll be staying."

"No, I'm just leaving." Penny slipped by so fast Charlie didn't have a chance to catch her. Before she went out the door, she sent a regretful look over her shoulder. "I'm so sorry. I should've stayed away."

Was she saying *this* was her fault?

Charlie took a deep breath, and then let it out. Granted, it was bad timing, but his crew's defection had nothing to do with her. "Penny, wait!"

"Mr. Hardt, hear me out. Now might be a good time to consider my uncle's offer."

Percy's remark stopped Charlie dead in his tracks. He turned and advanced on the land agent. "Was this *your* idea to tell the men about a gold strike? So you and your uncle can get your paws on the mine?"

"No, not at all!" Percy scrambled away and went behind the bar. "I told you, someone came to town. A stranger. No one knows him."

"But they believed him?" Charlie pushed up his coat sleeve. He hated sniveling cowards. He hated liars even more.

Percy pointed to the door. "Ask the men still outside. *They'll* tell you!"

Scowling, Seamus caught Percy by his checkered coat sleeve. "Get your yeller tail out from behind me bar and face the mayor like a man."

The scrawny land agent held his hat in front of him like a shield. "I-I thought I was doing you a *favor* by coming in here to tell you the news. But I can see you don't appreciate it."

Hell, maybe Percy wasn't lying. Could be it happened exactly like he said, and the men had moved on to greener pastures. Happened every day in mining towns.

Charlie dropped his arm. He'd find other men willing to work for him, or he'd blast the tunnels himself. In the meantime, he would go after Penny. Noelle wasn't that big, she couldn't get far. He walked past the land agent on his way out the door. "The marriage deal is still on."

PENNY RAN from the saloon past the bank. She wobbled on the boards that served as a walkway, feeling a bit strange and out-of-joint. Was this the effect of the whiskey? She shouldn't have asked for a second drink, much less finished it. Then again, that might've been Charlie's plan, to take advantage of her weakened willpower. He *had* offered another proposal, and he'd tricked her before.

She threw a frantic look over her shoulder. He hadn't followed yet, and maybe he wouldn't. He might decide to go after his men instead, now that he realized what an albatross she could be. But she had to find a place to hide in case he did happen to decide to come look for her.

When she came to the diner she tried the door, then ducked inside.

A delicious smell made her mouth water and Penny realized she hadn't eaten since breakfast. She looked around with surprise at the empty tables, and during lunchtime no less.

Loud voices came from the back, and it sounded as if they were speaking Spanish.

"Hello?" Penny called out.

Fina appeared in a back doorway, wearing an apron stained with what appeared to be tomatoes, and that long knife she wielded was meant for cutting up vegetables, hopefully.

"Are you open?"

"Yes, of course!" Fina set the knife aside on a table and came over to Penny, greeting her with a hug. "How are you? I saw the mayor carrying you into the saloon."

This wasn't a topic Penny wanted to discuss.

"I'm all right. But Mr. Hardt isn't very happy right now. His crew left town for some new gold strike."

"I heard about that. The restaurant cleared out too."

Penny blinked. The room seemed to be tilting. Her stomach did a slow flip and she swallowed fast. "Do you mind if I sit down?"

"Come over here. I'll get you something to eat."

Penny followed Fina to the first table. She shed her gloves, cloak and scarf. "I just need a place to sit for a little while. But I'll gladly pay for a plate of food."

"Don't worry about it if you're not hungry. You can stay as long as you like."

"Thank you." Penny slumped on her elbows, feeling miserable. Her friend would think she was horrible for wanting to leave, especially now that the miners had cleared out, but she couldn't take the risk of staying and marrying Charlie, even if she wanted to. His good luck might not be strong enough to stand up against her misfortune, which was why she'd left the gold nugget necklace he'd given her on the table back at the saloon. He needed all the help he could get.

Fina plopped onto the opposite bench. "Hey, I've

got some salve for those scratches."

Penny's hand went to her neck. Why hadn't she remembered to keep her scarf on? "They don't hurt that much. It's just so humiliating."

"What?" Fina slapped her hands on the table. "No, no. *You* should be *proud* of yourself. All the other ladies agree with me."

"Truly? You aren't embarrassed to be around me?"

"We're *glad* you popped Betsey in the nose. Someone needed to."

Penny sighed with relief. Back east, she would've had to go into seclusion for months. Charlie hadn't acted embarrassed either. After he'd come to her aid, he had seen to her needs, very tenderly. "Mr. Hardt was kind to help me."

Fina's lips curved in a knowing smile. "You gonna marry the mayor?"

Penny dropped her head into her hands, heart sore and confused. "I don't know, Fina. I *want* to." It was relief to finally admit the truth. "But I'm afraid to risk it."

"He might help you make up your mind. I see him coming this way."

Penny ducked down onto the bench so she wouldn't be visible through the window in front. She wasn't ready to face him. "Did he see me?"

"No, I don't think so. He's gone past. You can sit up."

Maybe Charlie hadn't been coming after her. Why did that thought make her even more miserable? Her eyes began to sting. Knowing tears would follow, she turned her face away and pretended to be looking at the colorful murals painted on the wall.

"*Chiquita*. Tell me what's wrong. I think you like our mayor, maybe more than like him. Why can't you marry him?"

What could Fina do, except give her sympathy and cards with saints on them? Then again, it might help to unburden her soul. Penny took a breath and slowly let it out to help her regain her composure. "You remember the card you gave me?"

"*Sí.*"

"You said it would ward off evil spirits. I don't think it worked. There's something wrong with me, Fina, something that brings bad luck to others. Especially the men I marry. I fear my love is deadly."

That sounded ridiculous, even to her ears. Nonetheless, she was afraid.

"I know what you need." Fina's declaration took Penny by surprise.

"You do?"

Fina reached across the table and took her hand, giving it a squeeze. "My grandmother was a *curandera*. She would advise if you believe the bad luck resides within you, make an herbal bath in the name of *Santa Muerte* and light white candles, one with *Huesuda* etched on it, unless you have a statue of her?"

Penny shook her head slowly. She brushed at a dirty spot on her sleeve and finally gave up. She'd need to wash everything. Herself included. "You think I need a bath?"

"No, not just a bath, it must be a *cleansing* bath. You should use sage." Fina twisted on the bench. "Nacho! *¿Tenemos salvia?*"

"*Si!*" Her husband's answer came from the kitchen. "*¿Para cocinar un pollo?*"

"No, not for chicken. It's for Señora Jackson."

After a moment, Nacho emerged from the kitchen. He put a fragrant bundle of sage bound with string on the table and gave Penny a friendly smile. His gaze moved from her to Fina and then back again, bright with curiosity. "This is what you need?"

"*Gracias*, now you can leave us. I'll be back to help you soon." Fina patted his arm.

Nacho leaned down and brushed a kiss on his wife's cheek. "*Esperaré una eternidad.*"

Her gaze softened as she looked up at him, and she toyed with a shiny dark braid hanging over her shoulder. "You won't have to wait *that* long."

The heated look they exchanged made translation unnecessary.

Uncomfortable, Penny averted her gaze. Would she ever share that kind of easy intimacy with someone? Charlie had given her a taste of soaring passion, but he hadn't offered her love. She ought not expect it. He was only rushing to marry her to meet a deadline.

"Now, we need to find two white candles and a ribbon," Fina mused. "Give me a few minutes to get everything together. Nacho will give you something to eat while you wait."

Penny stood. This was starting to sound like hocus-pocus. "Thank you, but no."

"*Chiquita*, you asked for my help." Fina propped her hands on her hips. "I am telling you what you need to do, and I know it will work. But if you keep holding onto the bad luck, you won't get rid of it."

In a sense, Charlie had told her the same thing. At least this was an action she could take, however far-fetched. And if it worked, it might give him extra protection.

Fina held up the bundle of dried sage. "Are you ready to send the bad luck away?"

Penny considered her options. "Where will I go to have this bath?

CHAPTER 11

*O*f all places, Fina had to pick the cathouse for the *cleansing bath*.

"*La Maison* has the largest bathtub in town," she explained, as Penny followed her upstairs to the second floor. "Pearl told me it was shipped in all the way from New York."

"I don't care where it came from." Penny shuddered to think about the kind of gossip her being there would elicit. Granted, she had lived here with the other eleven brides after the sheriff had temporarily evicted the residents. But now that most of the women were married, it would no doubt go back to being a brothel.

"No one will catch us. I told Nacho to tell the mayor that you went back to his cabin to get your bag. Aggie is here with Pearl, and they promised to keep watch."

"I can't believe Aggie will be living here much longer." Penny bit her lip. *No.* She'd promised not to tell anyone about Gus and Aggie's secret romance.

"She's seeing old Gus, but I don't think she's ready to marry him."

"You know? He said it was a secret."

Fina threw an incredulous look over her shoulder. "Nobody can keep a secret in this town."

Penny didn't mention she hadn't known until Gus told her yesterday. She should've been more aware. Or maybe no one trusted her not to mess things up.

"Why won't she marry him?"

"Maybe she thinks he's too old."

"She's older than him!"

Fina shrugged. "Maybe she thinks *she's* too old."

Penny shook her head. That pretty well ended the hope of Aggie taking her place, at least in time to meet the deadline. This bath had better work.

In the madam's bedroom, a strong scent lingered; the perfume she wore in copious amounts. The brass bed's satin coverlet had been thrown back, along with the sheets and blankets, as if someone had gotten out of bed and hadn't looked back. Odd paraphernalia lay scattered on the bed stand, including several medicine bottles. The door to the wardrobe stood open, revealing garish gowns hung on hooks.

"She must've moved back the minute we vacated the premises," Penny whispered.

"How come you're whispering? She's locked up in the jail."

Fina pulled the heavy velvet curtains closed. The only light came from the flickering flames of three white tapers on the dressing table.

"Good, Aggie found candles." Fina wrapped a ribbon around one. "I already wrote the petition, and she carved the image from a card I gave her."

Penny eyed the claw-foot tub in the corner of the room. "So all I have to do is bathe?"

"Wait, one more thing." Fina dug into the flour sack she'd slung over one shoulder and removed the bundle of sage. She used one of the candles to light the end.

A strong, earthy fragrance filled the room, as did smoke, which made Penny cough.

This had to be one of the craziest things she'd ever done. But she had tried everything else—regular prayers for years, throwing salt over her shoulder, living with a cricket in her house, removing her hair from her brush and burning it. Nothing had worked. Still, she had to try again, if she were to have any hope of helping Charlie, without making his situation worse.

After the sage smoldered for a moment, Fina smudged ashes around the inside of the tub. "I think that'll do it."

"You don't know?"

"I never really did this before. But my *abuela* told me all about it, and I mostly remember. All right, now get in the tub."

Being modest, Penny turned her back to unbutton her jacket. She had shared a room with three other women, now married, but she still felt shy undressing in front of others.

Fina made her way around the room again, smudging more ashes on the furniture, on the walls, and even some around the door. "You bathe while the candles burn down. It's good to pray to *Santa Muerte* because all life ends in death, and she can kill any evil coming her way."

Penny stepped into the tub and sat down, shivering. The air in the room was smoky, but still cold, and the lukewarm water didn't quite reach her knees. She stared with consternation at a crimson robe tossed over a chair next to the bed. "Does it strike you odd to be using this place to perform a sacred ceremony?"

"Where you do it doesn't matter. *La Muerte*

accepts people as they come. Rich, poor, old, young…we all end in dust. Or ashes to ashes, as your custom says."

"Or up in smoke." Penny coughed and waved her hand in front of her face. The haze in the room and the scent was almost overpowering. No wonder the evil spirits fled. They would suffocate otherwise.

"Now you're all set. All you have to do is pray." Fina picked up the sack and started for the door. "I told Nacho I'd help him finish preparing for the evening crowd. I'll be back soon."

"Wait! What do I say?"

"Whatever's on your heart."

"But how will I know if I'm doing it correctly?"

The door shut with a snick.

Penny wished that Fina might've stayed to add her prayers, which were bound to be more effective. Did saints even listen to Protestants? With a sigh, she leaned back. The smoke wasn't so thick anymore, and she was getting used to the smell. Might as well bathe first. *La Muerte* would appreciate supplications more from a clean woman than a dirty one.

She proceeded to wash dirt off her face and arms. If she had more time, and soap, she would thoroughly wash her hair, but that would take hours. She cleaned the ends and did her best to work out the tangles with her fingers. Cupping a handful of water, she dribbled it over her chest. The water and cold air combined to make her shiver, and her nipples constricted.

A bang resounded from somewhere below. Then she heard a murmur of voices, words she couldn't make out, followed by the sound of heavy footfalls on the stairs.

Penny sat forward. "Fina?"

"Stop! You can't go up there," shouted a woman who sounded like Pearl.

The heavy steps got louder, and then someone was knocking on the door.

Penny clambered out of the tub, almost slipping on the wood floor, and frantically looked around for something to use to cover herself. Why hadn't Fina left a bath sheet?

"Penny? Are you in there?"

Her alarm spiraled. *Charlie? What was he doing here?*

Her hands shook as she grabbed her shift off the bed. If she was quiet, he might assume the room was empty and go away.

The glass doorknob turned. *Oh good Lord! It wasn't locked!*

Panicked, Penny tossed the shift aside, grabbed the silk robe on the chair and pulled it on.

Less than a second later, Charlie stood in the open doorway.

"Get out!" she cried, wrapping the gown around her.

Surprise flashed across his face, but then he narrowed his eyes. Rather than leaving, he stepped inside and shut the door behind him. His gaze swept the room, returning to travel over her, from head to toe and back up again.

"What the *hell* is going on?" he demanded.

What did he *think* she was doing? Entertaining a customer?

He scrunched his nose. "What's that smell?"

If she started screaming, would it help? No. Then the whole town would know. Best to remain calm and get rid of him.

"Sage. I'm performing a cleansing. I'd like to get back to it, if you don't mind."

"You ran away from me so you could take a *bath*?"

The door swung open, and Pearl stuck her head in. "Mr. Hardt, you have to leave!"

Charlie spun around and pushed her back out into the hall. "No, *you* leave. I have business to discuss with Mrs. Jackson." He closed the door and locked it.

Penny groaned. Now he'd made matters worse. *Much* worse.

"I'm going for Draven," Pearl shouted.

"You do that," Charlie answered. "And when you come back, bring the preacher with you."

~

WHAT WAS PENNY HIDING? Well, besides a beautiful body, and the damp robe didn't hide *that* very well. He jerked his gaze to her face. "We need to have a talk about our future."

Her eyes flashed silver. "Surely, we can talk *after* I have a chance to get dressed?"

If he left, she'd just find another way to avoid him, or she'd make sure other people were around. He'd gotten as far as the freight house when he realized he'd been duped. Penny wouldn't have gone to his cabin. She'd leave town in a dirty dress before she'd risk getting caught alone with him again. Too bad, because he was keeping her here until she agreed to marry him.

"Are you finished with your bath? You can put on your clothes." He should probably offer to turn around.

With a peeved frown, she hugged her chest. "I'm

not just taking a bath. It's a ceremony to get rid of evil."

Her response shook him a little. "I know I can be a pest, but I'm not evil."

"The cleansing is for *me*, not *you*."

Charlie couldn't believe what he was hearing. "You don't have evil inside you, Penny."

"The curse then, bad luck, whatever you want to call it."

He took a step forward, longing to close the distance between them and take her into his arms and make her forget all about this superstitious nonsense that had her so scared. "Darlin' you aren't any more cursed than I am, and I can guarantee you I have more reason to be *cleansed*."

Uncertainty flashed across her face, but then her eyes pleaded. "Pearl is fetching the sheriff. Are you bound and determined to ruin me?"

He removed his hat and drove his fingers through his hair in pure frustration. "No! That's not what I want. But you keep running away every time I try to talk to you. Look here, just agree to marry me then I'll go downstairs and wait for you to get dressed."

Penny turned away from him, but not before he saw her gaze fill with hopelessness. She was going to refuse him. Again.

He didn't have time to ponder her reasoning, and

wooing her with words wasn't working. There was only one way to get through to her.

Crossing the room in two strides, he took her by the shoulders and spun her around, dragged her to him, then silenced her gasp with a kiss.

In less than a heartbeat, her lips softened. A moment later, her hands crept up his chest and she circled her arms around his neck, tangling her fingers in his hair. Then she kissed him like the house was on fire.

Ah, this was *his* Penny, an intoxicating blend of fiery passion and sweet vulnerability.

He stroked his hands down her back and over the slight flare of her hips beneath the silky robe. Her natural form was slender, delicate, and softly curved. Perfect.

Lost in passion, he hardly registered the rattling of the door.

"Hey there, open up."

Draven.

Charlie considered drawing his gun and shooting through the door. He loosened his hold on Penny, only slightly, but she took the opportunity to push him away, and ran to hide behind a silk screen painted with erotic scenes.

The sheriff pounded on the door. "You all right in there?"

"I'm fine." Charlie replied dryly.

"Mrs. Jackson? You want me to break in?"

A horrified gasp came from behind the screen. "Do something!" she whispered.

All right, enough was enough. Penny wouldn't come out from behind the screen and Draven, curse his innards, wasn't going away until he knew she was safe.

Charlie went to the door and turned the key until the latch clicked.

"Not *that!*" Penny cried.

He opened the door.

"Where is she?" Draven peered around him.

"Behind the screen. Penny, tell the nice sheriff you're all right."

"I'm fine, thank you. Mr. Hardt was just leaving."

Oh no. He wasn't going anywhere without her. That kiss had convinced him she wanted him as much as he wanted her, and *want* was enough for now. They'd work out the other details later.

Charlie smiled and forced a lighter tone to his voice. "Nah, I think I'll stay here and wait for you while you finish dressing, *sweetheart*. Sheriff Draven can let the reverend know we'll meet him at the saloon in, say, half an hour? That ought to give you enough time to get ready for our wedding."

CHAPTER 12

*R*everend Hammond had managed to gather up a respectable crowd for the impromptu wedding. The lanterns hanging from the saloon's rafters illuminated expressions ranging from elation to curiosity. The knot in Penny's chest tightened when she met Fina's questioning gaze.

The bath had been interrupted before it had time to work its magic. If indeed there was any chance it offered a mystical cure, which Penny doubted. She could count on nothing to reassure her she was doing the right thing by marrying Charlie.

Granted, she could've turned him down in spite of the subsequent humiliation. Scoundrel that he was, he deserved to be served a piece of humble pie.

But that would mean abandoning him when time was running out.

"Congratulations, you two!" Reverend Hammond shook Charlie's hand, looking mighty smug. The last time he'd suggested marriage, Charlie had choked him.

Felicity hovered at her husband's side. She offered Penny a hug. "I'm so happy for you. You're getting a very good man."

"Sometimes he can be good," Penny murmured. Other times, she wanted to kill him.

Oh no, that's not what she wanted. She took it back before Fate could register the request.

Charlie tucked her hand in the crook of his arm, in a sense, anchoring her to him. Was he afraid she'd run again? All he had to do was kiss her, and she forgot all about the reasons she *should* run. So she had stopped running and let him catch her. He would get what he wanted—the railroad built through Noelle—and she would get what she wanted. Charlie. God help him.

"Are we ready?" the reverend asked.

"Absolutely," Charlie replied.

Penny smiled. He never seemed to lack for confidence, so she would borrow a little. She nodded.

The conversations around them died down and the room grew silent. So quiet she could hear the wind buffeting the building. Another winter storm must be brewing.

The preacher opened his Bible. "We're gathered here today on this happy occasion to see these two wed." He arched an eyebrow at Charlie. "It's about time."

A low titter rippled through the crowd.

"Dearly beloved," Reverend Hammond boomed.

A loud bang made Penny flinch.

"Shut the door!" the barkeeper shouted. "Yer lettin' in the cold."

"Oh, sorry about that," the intruder replied in a cultured tone.

Penny twisted to look. She knew that voice. Mr. Montgomery.

The Englishman removed his hat and unwound his scarf, looking confused as he surveyed the gathering. "I seem to have interrupted something."

"I'd say." His wife Minnie hurried back to where he stood near the door. "Where have you been? I left a note for you to meet me here."

"Didn't see it. I was testing a sample of galena that Mrs. Jackson gave me, and I came over straightaway to see if I could find Mr. Hardt to tell him the results."

"You can tell me later." Charlie shouted. "Take a

seat or stand there by the bar. We're getting married."

Penny couldn't move when Charlie took her arm in an attempt to turn her to face the preacher. Shock held her immobile. What were the chances the assayer would show up *at this moment*? It had to be some kind of sign. She dared not ignore it. "Tell us, what did you find?"

Charlie rolled his eyes. "Oh, good grief. It can wait."

In her heart, she longed to turn her back on the interruption and continue on as if nothing had happened. They could find out after they were married. But that would be an act of pure selfishness. If this marriage wasn't necessary, they needed to know *before* he committed the rest of his life. "I think we should let Mr. Montgomery share his news before we proceed."

Penny trained her attention on the assayer so she wouldn't have to see Charlie's disapproving frown. In a moment, he might not be so angry.

Mr. Montgomery darted a glance at her groom and nodded once. Charlie gave him the go ahead. "Those tailings you gave me, I didn't find much gold, but I did find significant traces of silver. I knew it wouldn't be enough to warrant excitement, not unless we could track it back to the source. The rock you gave Mrs. Jackson, the one from the old mine, it contained a substantial quantity of silver. I think you may have found the source."

Charlie's face reflected stunned disbelief. "How substantial?"

"You could be sitting on a fortune."

Gasps went up around the room, and then everyone began to converse in excited whispers.

Penny closed her eyes and fought to maintain her composure. Hadn't she suspected something might happen? Fate had once again intervened and squelched her hopes.

Ironically, Charlie was surprisingly lucky. If he could walk into that meeting tomorrow and announce a big silver strike, the railroad board would fall all over themselves in their hurry to complete the line. And he would be spared an unnecessary, and unwanted marriage.

She forced calmness in her expression, in spite of the agonizing ache in her chest and burning in her throat. "What wonderful news. It appears the town will be saved, thanks to you, Charlie."

When she tried to remove her hand from his arm, he held on. Maybe he didn't understand, or it hadn't hit him yet. "This certainly changes things. I don't believe we need to go on."

Everyone in the room had gone silent, as if they were collectively holding their breath.

He glowered at her. "Are you backing out?"

"I'm giving you your freedom."

"What if I say I want to finish what we started?"

She could hardly believe he would, considering his adamant objections before yesterday and his reasoning for wanting to marry her in the first place. Perhaps he needed to be absolutely certain the railroad deal would go through. "Very well. Why don't you go with Mr. Montgomery and check out what he's discovered? Depending on what you find, you may change your mind."

His features hardened like they were carved in hard rock quartz. But he finally let go of her hand. "Wait here. I'll be back."

CHARLIE TOOK long strides as he left the saloon, fighting to control his anger. He wanted to shake Penny, or toss her over his shoulder and head straight for the cabin without further conversation. They communicated much better in bed. He decided it would be best if he took a break and cooled off so he wouldn't lose his temper and yell at her.

Hugh kept pace, wisely mentioning nothing

about Penny's defection. "I've tested that one sample. I'd like to test more."

"They're in the back of my wagon up at the cabin. Take some of those as samples. I'll go retrieve the dynamite I unloaded yesterday. We'll need it to bring more of that rock out of the old mine. Let's meet back here in an hour. That ought to give Mrs. Jackson enough time to make up her mind."

He parted with Hugh at the corner and started up the same path he'd descended earlier.

Silver. Who knew?

His luck with mining thus far had been better than his luck with women.

Penny confused him. Was she worried whether he'd be rich enough to take care of her? That would explain why she took the rock to the assayer in the first place. He hadn't thought wealth mattered much to her. But he'd been wrong about another woman, stupidly infatuated and blind to her faults until it was too late. Only...Penny hadn't agreed to marry him thinking she'd be rich. In fact, she'd tried her hardest to dissuade him.

His sense of certainty wavered. He'd all but dragged Penny in front of a preacher, assuming it was fear that held her back. Maybe fear wasn't the only reason she resisted.

His lungs were burning by the time he reached

the entrance. This tight, painful throbbing in the center of his chest was due to exertion. *Not* rejection.

He put his hand on a thick crossbeam shoring up the entrance and leaned over to listen. Generally, he heard noises coming from inside: the pinging of pickaxes, squeaky wheels on rails, men singing or cursing. Today he heard...nothing.

Percy had been right. The crew was long gone.

Charlie had gotten past his initial anger, and he had to admit, hurt feelings. Even after being betrayed by people close to him, he still thought loyalty begat loyalty. As it turned out, it was all about money. Would the men have stayed if he'd increased their pay? As it was, he barely had enough to cover their salaries, and he'd drained his savings, pouring money back into the mine. He'd been careful about seeking out investors because of his former partner's duplicity, and he didn't trust Percy's uncle after reading about all the railroad scandals. He refused to risk losing control over the mine, watching some rich Easterner take away the earnings that were meant to sustain Noelle.

He had to hunch over as he entered the narrow tunnel, one disadvantage of being taller than most of the miners who worked for him. He stopped to retrieve a miner's candlestick wedged in between a crevice and lit the candle.

Further back, he came to a drift. Not far from where the men had been blasting. The area where he was sure they would find another rusty vein of quartz. His instincts had been off. This mine was played out when it came to gold. He hadn't paid enough attention to its potential for silver. If Penny hadn't trusted her instincts, he'd still be wasting his time chasing his tail. He owed her for that, and he would see to it that she got everything she wanted.

The tunnel opened into a cavernous space where he could stand upright, which was much more comfortable. He lifted the candlestick and saw only bare floor.

Where were the dynamite charges? He'd left them here early yesterday, along with the tools, hammer and drill-bits. Had that disloyal pack of coyotes made off with everything? If so, he would round up those son-of-a-guns and hang their sorry hides from the nearest tree.

Still swearing, Charlie turned and headed back the way he'd come. He hadn't gone far before a startling wave of cold halted him in his tracks. He used his free hand to hug his arm. If he didn't know better, he would think someone had opened a window and let in a Blue Norther. Only, there wasn't a window in the mine, and this cold sensation wasn't exactly wind.

Something—he shuddered—*someone* moved right through him!

Every hair on the back of his neck stood on end. *What the hell?*

A boom shook the floor beneath his feet, followed by a loud rumble.

He braced his hand against the rocky wall for support while holding tight to the miner's candlestick so he wouldn't drop it and be left entirely in darkness.

As the rumbling subsided, small chunks of rock broke free and bounced onto the floor of the cave. The cold seeped through his skin, feeling like ice water in his veins.

CHAPTER 13

*A*t the saloon, Penny waited. Growing cold, she'd taken a seat close to the pot-bellied stove. The other ladies offered to stay with her, but she told them to go on and she would send word when Charlie came back. The saloon cleared out quickly after that, except for a few stragglers—

Genevieve, and her new husband; the preacher, who insisted there would still be a wedding; and his wife, who didn't look quite so sure.

Genevieve drummed her fingers on the table. "Mr. Hardt will return, and he *will* marry you. I know this is what he wants. I could see it in his eyes."

Penny couldn't speak without getting choked up, so she just nodded. She'd seen promises in Charlie's eyes too, as well as heat and hunger, passion and possessiveness, exquisite tenderness, even affection. But she had learned the hard way not to embrace hope too quickly.

She swallowed and recovered her voice. "What Charlie *wants* is to save this town. He felt he didn't have a choice except to marry me. Now, it appears he has a choice."

"He made his choice. You'll see." Reverend Hammond set his drink on the table and swung a chair around, his usual smile firmly in place, if a little frayed around the edges.

"I hope so." Penny slid a furtive look at the door. Would Charlie take the chance to get away while he still could and not tempt fate?

A distant boom resounded.

The preacher came to his feet. "What was that?"

"Sounds like they're blastin' again." Mr. Malone dragged a rag across the bar with a disgusted look on his face.

Penny's hopes sank. Charlie had immediately gone to work, which would make sense if he wanted to bring hard evidence of a silver strike to the meeting tomorrow. She curled her hands in her lap and dug her nails into her palms to distract from the pain searing the inside of her chest. This was what she expected, what *should* happen, so she had no reason to feel crushed. Now she should go. He had made his choice.

She moved her chair back.

No!

Charlie's command, though only a voice in her head, arrested her in the midst of her spiraling dive into despair. Charlie hadn't run out on her. She had sent him away. Yet every time she pushed him aside, or managed to evade him, he came back. His stubborn refusal to give up was one of the things she loved most about him. She owed him this chance to find out what he truly wanted. Either way, he would be back to tell her.

"I'll wait."

The next moments crept by slowly.

The door swung open, letting in a swirl of cold wind and snowflakes.

Her heart leapt.

Charlie?

A man bundled in a heavy coat and scarf stepped inside. Mr. Montgomery jerked his scarf down and his panicked expression sent a shaft of fear through her chest. "There's been an accident, a cave-in. Mr. Hardt's trapped in the mine!"

DUST CLOGGED in Charlie's nose and throat. He coughed. He'd gotten back through the tunnels leading to the entrance without a problem, but a wall of rocks blocked the exit. If he had come back here minutes, no *seconds*, earlier, he would've been buried underneath the rubble.

His skin prickled.

That strange cold sensation had stopped him.

He held up the candle and surveyed the damage. What had caused the tunnel to cave in? It had sounded like an explosion, but no one was around to set charges, and they wouldn't blast near the entrance anyway. He'd checked the supports yesterday and everything looked fine. Well, *something* went wrong. If there were clues, he'd missed them. Just like the last time.

Three years ago, in the midst of setting charges inside the old mine, something had gone terribly wrong. Back then, Zeke Kinnison had been his foreman leading the best crew he'd ever had, which included Zeke's brother. By the time Charlie reached the mine, Zeke had been a wild man, tearing away the rock until it shredded his bare hands, in a frantic effort to get to his brother. They'd retrieved Clem's broken body hours later.

Charlie forced the image out of his head. He couldn't let his mind go there, or he'd lose it, which was a sure way to get killed. He wedged the pointed end of the miner's candlestick into a crevice in the wall and pulled the scarf up over his nose to keep from breathing dust.

The candle's flame cast eerie shadows over the dense wall of rock between him and freedom. He had, at best, two hours before the taper burned out.

Better get to work.

He hefted a large rock. The subsequent *creak* made him freeze. A few loosened pebbles rattled to the floor.

Sweet Jesse.

If he wasn't careful, the roof and walls might give way right on top of him.

He selected another chunk of stone that appeared safe to dislodge. Working carefully, he treated the obstacle like a puzzle, keeping his attention focused on the task.

Within minutes, he was sweating profusely. Clearing all this rock would, realistically, take a crew, and they would have to work slowly, shoring up the walls and the roof as they went, so as not to trigger another cave-in.

Panting, he leaned his hand against the wall. The air was getting thin, he'd made little progress, and there was no way of knowing how bad things were at the entrance.

By now, Hugh would've gone for help. And Penny? Knowing her, she'd be consumed with guilt and would have some harebrained notion that this was her fault. Admittedly, she'd been passed by when the powers that be were handing out good fortune. But if he was destined to die, it would be because of stupidity or past sins.

He shouldn't have let her stop the wedding. That had been a mistake. Her retreat signaled fear more than disinterest, and he should've guessed that would happen when he got close to victory.

She thought he wanted his freedom more than he wanted her. Maybe he could've fooled himself into believing that, if he weren't stuck underground, facing his own mortality. How ironic, for the first time in years, he felt fully alive. Being with Penny had reawakened his desires and hopes. She'd given him a reason to look forward to the future.

He wouldn't have a future if he didn't get the hell out of here.

Another option came to mind. It was a slim chance, but still possible. If he could find that tunnel, he would have a way out. But to reach it, he had to descend to a lower level, using one of the ore buckets.

If he dropped the candle, he'd be in total darkness. On the other hand, if he stayed here, he could be waiting in darkness for days before they dug him out. Then, when they started clearing the unstable entrance, it might collapse further, burying and killing all of them. Regardless, time was running out. After the candle melted, the choice would be made for him.

He couldn't afford to sit and wait.

CAVE-IN. *Charlie. Dear Lord.* Penny trembled from a chill that had nothing to do with the wind whirling into the saloon through the open door. She didn't feel the cold. She felt nothing except an icy fist squeezing her heart.

A distant, yet loud clanging started up.

"There's the alarm. Good, Woody sounded it. I have to go help the others." The assayer spun around and went back outside.

Penny followed Mr. Montgomery, grabbing her cloak on the way out the door. "What happened?"

The clanging continued. People came running out of shops and stores. Penny had to sprint to keep up with the assayer's long strides so she could hear his answer.

"I went up to the cabin to get those other samples. Charlie told me he was going to the mine to collect dynamite for later and said he'd meet me back here in an hour. Then I heard an explosion. When I got there, the entrance was caved in."

Two men commandeered donkey carts. The shopkeeper threw shovels and pick axes onto a long sled the blacksmith had brought around.

Mr. Montgomery swung up into his saddle, then reached down to help the doctor mount behind him. Their horse took off at a gallop, sending dirty snow airborne, splattering Penny's dress.

She headed toward the mountain. She had to get to Charlie. Save him. If necessary, dig him out with her bare hands.

"Penny, wait!" Genevieve captured her elbow. "Come with us. We'll get there faster." She guided Penny to a sleigh. "Zeke was a foreman at the mine several years ago. Let him drive us. He'll know what to do."

The women settled into the sleigh, and Zeke guided the horses toward the mine.

Genevieve put her arm around Penny's shoulders. "We'll find him."

When they did, would he be alive?

Penny struggled to breath. "I shouldn't have stopped the ceremony. No, I should've *left* yesterday and never come back. I sent him up there."

"It was an accident, Penny," Genevieve said firmly. "This isn't your fault."

An eternity passed before they reached their destination. Beams supporting the mine entrance had collapsed like toothpicks and huge, jagged rocks clogged the tunnel.

Fear sucked the air out of Penny's lungs. How could anyone live through that?

Even Mr. Kinnison appeared stunned. When he turned to Genevieve, the resignation in his gaze was more than Penny could bear. "We'll need help. Food for the men and bandages, just in case."

"I'll go back and rally the women." Genevieve picked up the reins. Her husband left to help the other men, who were throwing rocks away from the entrance.

They might as well be tossing pebbles.

Penny climbed out of the sleigh and huddled in her cloak. She wasn't going anywhere, not until she knew Charlie was safe. After that, she would get as far away from him as possible. "I'll stay here and do what I can."

"Yes, I thought you might say that," Genevieve replied, her gaze soft with concern. "Ask one of the men for a pair of work gloves. You'll ruin the ones you have on."

Penny started toward a pile of rubble, passing a

brawny man who guided a team of burros that strained to dislodge a boulder. Charlie could be anywhere, behind—or God forbid—under that rock or the next.

Her chest tightened and she gulped air.

"Mrs. Jackson?"

Penny halted, belatedly realizing that she'd passed right by the doctor while he'd been hailing her. "I'm sorry, Dr. Deane. Is there something I can do for you?"

His concerned gaze traveled over her. "Go inside and get warm so I'll not have another patient to worry about."

"I rarely fall ill," she replied, honestly. It was one of the cruel ironies that her back luck didn't strike at her health, only the health of others. "And I refuse to see to my needs while everyone else works to free Mr. Hardt. I can move rocks too."

The doctor set his bag on the ground and solemnly regarded the monstrous task in front of them. "It appears that's all any of us can do at the moment."

No, that couldn't be all they could do. There had to be something else. Something they were missing. Charlie wouldn't have blown himself up, or set off dynamite without having a way out. He knew better than that. If this exit were blocked, he would be looking for another one.

Something he said the other day when they had stopped to the clear the rockslide…

"He said they'd blasted through," she whispered.

"Mr. Kinnison!" She called out as she ran towards him. "What if Charlie isn't in there? What if we're looking in the wrong place?

CHAPTER 14

*A*fter Penny told the men about the possibility of a connecting tunnel, they questioned her interpretation of Charlie's remark. Why would he have connected the two mines, one of which he considered useless? But she felt certain he'd meant exactly that, and she continued to pester them until Woody finally agreed to take her to the old mine, she assumed to keep her distracted more than anything. Zeke surprised her when he hopped into the back of the wagon at the last moment.

The sun had disappeared behind the tree line and the wind had picked up by the time they reached the pass. Penny used her hood to protect her face, while Woody guided the mule team to the edge of the rockslide.

She peered up at the old mine. Snow lay in patches across the desolate landscape. A stiff wind sent white whorls into the air. It was eerily quiet. Her heart stumbled. What if he wasn't here? "I remember Charlie saying they'd blasted through and it might've caused the rock slide."

"Could be," Mr. Kinnison replied. He still didn't appear to believe her. Or maybe he just wasn't hopeful. He had lost his brother to this mine, after all.

They'd brought lanterns, a canteen and snowshoes, which would be of no help climbing over those rocks.

"You ought to wait here, Mrs. Jackson," Woody suggested.

"I'm not sitting in the sleigh freezing my bustle off. I can help too."

All the others had remained behind to continue clearing the other entrance, expecting to find Charlie buried beneath the rubble.

Somehow, she would *know* if he was dead.

The men lagged behind to help her maneuver the deep drifts along the side of the trail. She glanced at the spot where the road had been torn away. "I slipped and fell there, and Charlie rigged up a rope and came down to save me."

"Penny!"

She jerked her head up, heart pounding, but she

didn't see anyone near the old mine. Was she imagining his voice? "That's Charlie! Did you hear him?"

"I sure did," Woody said in a hushed voice. "I hope it's not a ghost."

Suddenly, a man appeared from around a boulder, not far from the old mine entrance.

She pointed at the figure. "There!"

The man scrambled, nimble as a mountain goat, around the rocks. She couldn't see his face because his hat brim was pulled low, but—*oh thank God!*—she did recognize that buckskin coat.

"Charlie!" She set the lantern aside, and climbed the rocks in her eagerness to reach him. "He found a way out!"

"Mrs. Jackson, take care," Mr. Kinnison warned, as he came up beside her and grasped her arm. "Don't climb up there. It's too dangerous. Wait for him to come down."

She was done with waiting. She had to touch him to make sure he was real and not an apparition dreamed up by her desperate mind.

He braced his hand on a boulder and leapt over it. As he landed, the small rocks beneath his boots went spinning away.

"That's no ghost." Woody confirmed her thoughts, then whooped, slapping his hand on his thigh. "Zeke, she was right!"

Penny shook off Mr. Kinnison's hold and kept her eyes on Charlie as she scrambled over the rocks. She would get to him even if she had to crawl on her hands and knees. "Charlie!"

"Hold on there." Gravel crunched as he slid down next to her. He slipped his hands beneath her arms, lifting her, and then pulled her into his embrace.

She flung her arms around his neck. "Oh, Charlie, you're alive. I knew it—" Her voice cracked under an avalanche of emotions, and she couldn't hold back a sob.

Charlie had escaped death.

This time.

～

"PENNY, HONEY, DON'T CRY." Charlie held her tight, pressing her head against his shoulder. If she didn't stop weeping, he'd soon be blubbering right along with her. He cleared his throat, but his voice still came out hoarse. "I told you I'd come back."

Still keeping one arm around her, he reached out to shake Woody's hand. "Thanks for coming after me."

Woody's grin got wider. "Wasn't me. She's the one who said you'd be here. She threatened to steal either Zeke's sleigh or my wagon unless we brought her out."

The other man with her was the one that surprised Charlie. The day Zeke's brother had died, so had a strong friendship and Charlie hadn't known how to repair the damage. Zeke's gaze was trained up at the mine. "Mrs. Jackson believed there was a connecting tunnel. I didn't think it made sense."

"It happened a few months ago by accident, when we were searching for a new vein."

"Maybe it wasn't an accident," Zeke mused.

Charlie dug into his pocket and his fingers closed around metal. "Yeah, maybe not."

He hugged her closer. Forces he didn't understand had tried to come between them, and powers just as mysterious had saved him. Why, he would never know. "When I was in the mine, right before the cave in, I felt this cold sensation, and then it was like someone walked right through me. Felt so strange, it stopped me from going back. If I'd gotten as far as the entrance, I would've been buried under those rocks."

Penny's arms tightened around him, and Woody's mouth hung open.

Zeke's gaze didn't falter.

"There's more. In the old tunnel, I came across

this." Charlie pulled the oil-wick lamp out of his pocket and handed it to Zeke. "Recognize it?"

"That's a miner's lamp; the old kind they clipped onto their hats."

"You remember Clem said he lost his?"

Silently, Zeke examined the rusty lamp. He ran his thumb over the spout and gingerly touched the burned wick.

"I wouldn't have seen it if I hadn't been looking down to keep from tripping. It had enough oil in it I was able to light it with the last of my candle, and that's how I found my way out." Charlie took a deep breath. Yeah, it sounded crazy, but standing here whole and uninjured was just as improbable. "I reckon Clem saved my life."

Something shifted in Zeke's countenance, softening the hardness in his eyes as well as the tension that had been present between them ever since Clem's death. "I'm sure he was glad to get the opportunity."

"You keep that. It belonged to Clem."

Zeke handed it back to Charlie. "No, *you* keep it. Never know when you might need it again."

Penny's arms tightened around his waist. "He'll never need it again after I'm gone."

Charlie rubbed his hand on her back. Just as he'd feared, she was taking this all on herself. At least he didn't have to worry about whether she wanted him. The way she was clinging to him told him all he needed to know. "You aren't going anywhere."

She drew back with a heartbreaking expression of uncertainty tinged with hope. "But I can't risk your life again."

"Hush." He put his finger over her lips, which felt like ice. "You're cold. Let's get back to town."

He put his arm around her and guided her back to the sleigh then tucked the blanket around her. The two other men fell in behind them, lost in their own thoughts.

Woody took them around by the road back to the other mine, where Zeke hopped out to notify the others. The light had faded and if not for the lanterns they'd brought along, they would've been riding in darkness. Charlie draped his arm around Penny's shoulders and hugged her tightly to him. "Take us to The Golden Nugget. We've got some unfinished business."

Penny looked away. Her silence troubled him more than her objections.

As they pulled into town, the sheriff and doctor were standing outside the Doc's office beside a wagon. Draven hailed them and waved Woody over.

Colin Deane gave Charlie a hearty pat on the back as he stepped out of the sleigh. "Mr. Mayor, I should've known you'd cheat death. You've got better luck than an Irishman."

Charlie hoped Penny was paying attention.

"Mayor, good to see you alive." The sheriff shook his hand, and then motioned to the wagon bed. "We uncovered a body at the mine."

Behind him, Penny gasped.

Charlie's gut knotted. "One of my crew?"

Draven shook his head. "Nobody up there knows who he is. Maybe you could help us identify him." He turned back the blanket and the doctor lifted the lantern.

Light shone on a slender man in dust-coated clothing, miner's garb. Charlie's gaze halted at the man's hands, which had been crossed over his crushed chest. On his right hand, he wore a distinctive signet ring, embossed with a swirling C.

Charlie's arms broke out in gooseflesh. "Bring the light to his face."

He leaned closer to study the man's features. Bruised and battered, but still recognizable. "That's Robert Cortland."

"Cortland? Your former partner?" Penny scrambled out of the sleigh, but Charlie put his arm out and held her back.

"You don't want to see this."

The sheriff quickly flipped the blanket back over

the corpse. "Looks to me like he got caught under one of the supports. He had a stick of dynamite in his pocket. My guess is he set a charge somewhere in the tunnel and didn't get out in time."

"He tried to kill me once when he stole my gold." Charlie touched the old scar on his cheek. "Must've come back to finish the job." Whatever motive had compelled Cortland to return after all this time had died with him.

Charlie put his arm around Penny. "He's the one responsible for my bad luck, not you. Doc, put him on ice, then you and Draven come on over to the saloon. We're having a wedding."

CHAPTER 15

The street sparkled with light as the residents of Noelle turned out to welcome the mayor back and to witness a marriage between the twelfth couple. With the promised marriages finalized, along with the potential for silver, the railroad board would have no reason to dispute their agreement. Noelle would be saved.

Penny once again stood inside the door of the saloon, only this time she wasn't nervously clutching a piece of evergreen, wondering if her groom would show up.

Charlie was already there, waiting for her.

Her fears about bad luck had been mostly put to rest upon discovering a reason for the mine collapse. She had forced herself to set aside her doubts.

Charlie had asked for her trust, and perhaps with time, he would come to love her as much as she loved him.

The glow from an elk horn chandelier cast a gleaming hue over the rough-hewn walls and floors. Her groom's hair, which had been combed and smoothed down, shone like spun gold. Standing next to him—his best friend and the town's pastor—Chase Hammond clutched a Bible to his chest and beamed like a proud papa.

"This calls for a celebration. Whiskey for everyone!" Seamus Malone marched over to the bar. "The preacher's paying, ain't that right?"

"No I recall very clearly you said if we found him, the drinks would be on the *house*," Chase replied. "*After* the wedding."

Charlie smiled at Penny. "I'll cover the tab. We can toast my bride."

The ladies who'd arrived with her twelve days past—which in some ways seemed like a lifetime ago—gathered around her. Their husbands scrambled for chairs, a few sat on tables. Draven, Storm and the doctor stood with their elbows propped on the bar. Thankfully, the Thorntons had left their goose at home.

Genevieve pressed two decorative hairpins in

Penny's hand. "Use them to secure your veil. For good luck."

Zee Daniels handed her cherub-cheeked baby to her husband, Culver. The brawny blacksmith smiled indulgently when little Jem grabbed his nose with a gleeful squeal. The sound stirred a maternal longing in Penny's heart. She hadn't asked Charlie whether he wanted children, and he'd been so devastated when he lost his daughter, but she wondered if another child might help his heart heal.

"I have something for you too." Zee slipped a silver bracelet around Penny's wrist. "This was passed down from my great-grandmother. It's given me luck and protection."

"Oh Zee, thank you." Penny studied the pattern, which was possibly gypsy symbols or an ancient language. The precious gift touched her heart. "Are you sure you want to part with it?"

"I have more." Zee stepped back and looked Penny over, and her dark gaze warmed with approval. "That dress fits you perfectly."

"It does, doesn't it?" Penny smoothed her hands over the dress Charlie had sent Aggie to purchase for her, after she'd used the excuse she couldn't be married in soiled clothing. By some miracle, Gus must've remembered the dress she'd admired, because that was the one the elderly widow had returned with.

Birdie stood on tiptoe to attach the lacy veil to Penny's hair. "Something else you should know. This lace was made on a loom that was smuggled into France by one of the lace makers in Calais, so they could produce the kind of lace that the duke wished to give to his bride."

"Really?" Penny lifted her hands to the delicate fabric. She felt awful about how she'd treated the gift. "I can't believe you kept this for me."

"Why wouldn't I? I knew you'd have a use for it one day."

Humbled by her friend's thoughtfulness, Penny reached out to squeeze Birdie's hand. "Thank you. I don't deserve such kindness."

"Of course you do."

"Not after throwing this veil in your face."

Birdie's eyes twinkled as if she found the remark somehow funny. "As you said, you didn't need it then. But you do need it now."

Over her friend's shoulder, Penny spotted Grandpa Gus, who gave her an exaggerated wink. He nudged his grandson, Jack, who responded with a thumbs-up. They'd never acted afraid of her. They'd treated her as part of the family. And the other ladies, they'd stood by her, even when she'd doubted herself. In this way also, she was very lucky.

She stepped up beside Charlie.

The preacher opened his Bible. This time, he directed a pointed look at her. "Are we ready?"

"Yes," she said firmly.

"Just a minute."

Her heart shrank at Charlie's answer. Had he changed his mind?

He didn't look at her to reassure her. Rather, he seemed intent on digging something out of his coat pocket. He lifted her hand and placed it in her palm.

She stared in confusion at the little red drum, the last ornament in his collection. He'd stopped the ceremony because he'd forgotten to decorate the tree?

"The Drum and this ornament belong to you now. And I've already signed the papers. You'll own fifty percent interest in the mine—the gold, silver, whatever we take out of it."

"Wait!" A shout came from the near the door. "Stop! I object!"

~

CHARLIE TURNED AT THE INTERRUPTION. "What the devil?"

Percy elbowed his way through the crowd, ignoring the shocked and disapproving looks cast his direction. "You don't have the right to sign over half the mine. It doesn't belong to you."

As if a reluctant bride wasn't bad enough, they had to be interrupted again, and this time by a raving lunatic.

"You've been out in the sun too long, Penworthy. Go sit down."

The land agent's face flushed bright pink. He straightened the pince-nez at the end of his nose and adjusted his coat with a self-righteous sniff. "It's night, in case you haven't noticed. The preacher is going to ask if anyone has just cause to object, and *I* do. You can't offer your wife half interest in the mine without the approval of the other owner."

Either Percy was mad, or this was his way of getting control of the mine by perpetrating some sort of fraud.

Charlie stepped away from Penny and stalked the land agent. "What are you trying to pull?"

Looking alarmed, Percy moved his feet fast, scrambling in reverse, but he didn't get far before Draven gave him a push back toward Charlie, who snatched him up by the lapels of his tailored coat.

Charlie pinned him with an icy glare. "I smell a rat."

Percy squeaked, "Don't hit me! You...you'll break my glasses!"

"I don't hit rats. I feed them to my ferret."

The bean counter's eyelids fluttered.

"Don't you *dare* faint."

Percy's eyes snapped open, and he started sputtering. "I did nothing wrong. Mr. Cortland showed me a deed to the mine that had his name on it. He told us he'd found a fortune in silver, and he promised he would arrange for my uncle to buy into it. He-he'll be at the meeting tomorrow, you can talk to him about it then."

Silver... That would explain why Cortland had been sneaking around, and the rockslide too. He'd been awfully busy on the other side of the mountain, and Percy had kept his secret.

Charlie longed to wring the Judas's scrawny neck, and to think he'd *allowed* the slimy snake into his town. "You were doing business with Robert Cortland?"

Percy bobbed his head.

"He won't be attending any meetings," Draven ground out. "He's laid up over at Doc's—squashed flat as a bug."

"That's right," Charlie tightened his grip on Percy's coat. "Cortland set a charge at the mine entrance and blew it up. Tried to kill me. Reckon he thought if I was dead, no one would stand in his way."

Percy's face turned ashen. His mouth gaped open...closed...open—like a fish gasping for water. "I-I heard about the cave-in. But I *swear* I didn't know that was his plan. H-He didn't tell me *how* he would arrange things."

That was the sorriest excuse yet.

"He showed you a false deed. I bought him out three years ago. But you've been having fun, haven't you, running everybody in circles over these weddings, all along figuring you'd soon be getting rich off silver and running this town."

The fear in Percy's eyes confirmed Charlie's assumption. "No! You've got it wrong. I'm not that kind of person."

"I know exactly what kind of person you are. The kind that don't deserve to live."

The tension in the air was palpable, as Charlie coldly contemplated whether he could get away with murder.

A light touch on the back of his shoulder arrested him.

Penny.

He knew her touch without looking, because it stirred his heart and released a host of emotions that he'd tried, unsuccessfully, to bury. With just a touch, she reminded him his heart had once been soft. When it came to her, it was the consistency of pudding.

"Let him go, Charlie," she said softly. "The sheriff can deal with him."

He let go so fast Percy's knees gave way. The trembling agent would've collapsed if Draven hadn't caught hold of his arm.

"Lock him up," Charlie snapped. "He can explain it to the judge."

The sheriff's mauled brow twitched. "Our little jail's gettin' a mite crowded. You all must think I'm runnin' a hotel. Just in case this little mouse is tempted to run off, I'll find a spot for him. But he's not going anywhere until *after*."

"After what?" Charlie asked.

Draven cocked his head and wry amusement gleamed in his good eye. "After you marry that lady you been chasing all over town."

PENNY WATCHED in stunned amazement as the sheriff hauled the land agent to stand beside him while the ceremony commenced. Everyone else appeared equally surprised. There for a minute, she feared Charlie would wring the man's neck like he would a chicken's—not dissimilar to how he'd manhandled the preacher. The deceitful Mr. Penworthy deserved a good lashing, but then Charlie would be arrested.

Reverend Hammond, who'd backed off and rested his hip on the edge of a table, calmly observing the drama, came to his feet. "Well, that was exciting. Now…are we ready to continue?"

Charlie tucked her fingers over his arm and set his jaw. "I'm ready."

Penny lifted her other hand to look at the ornament, puzzled by what he meant in giving her half the mine. Was it because she'd asked for the rock to be assessed? Did he think that was why she'd finally agreed marry him, to become rich?

The reverend opened his Bible. "I'll pick up where I left off. Nah, let's get to the vows. Charles Augustus Hardt, do you take—"

"Excuse me, Reverend, I'd like to have a word with Mr. Hardt before we go on."

A thunderous expression darkened her groom's piercing gaze. "Do you, or don't you, want to get married?"

She tightened her hold on his arm. "If I didn't, I wouldn't be standing here."

Someone in the crowd barked a laugh, and

another person hushed him. She wasn't sure if Charlie's frown was meant for them or her.

"But I want to know why you think you need to give me this." She held up the ornament. "I don't need riches, Charlie. All I need is you."

He blinked down at her. His eyes looked a little glassy and then he cleared his throat. "That's good to know. But it seems I didn't make myself clear."

He clasped his hands on her shoulders. "Penny, I'm offering you ownership in the mine to show you that *you're* the only treasure I care about."

His treasure? Her? That meant his dogged pursuit hadn't only been about saving the town. Charlie *loved* her. That's what he was saying, and in the sweetest way possible.

In her heart, something felt like a key turned in a lock and a door opened. *The curse.* It was broken. Or maybe, as Charlie had claimed repeatedly, there had never been a curse, only fear, and his love had driven it out.

Elated, she threw her arms around his neck. "I love you, Charlie, more than anything, and I promise to honor and obey you... Well, to be honest, I'm not sure I'll always obey, but I can promise to trust you. And I'll never forsake you, in sickness or in health, as long as I live."

He tightened his embrace. "Penny Jackson..." His

voice quivered. "I pledge to honor and protect you, and to love and cherish you until death do us part."

From behind her came sounds of sniffling, and Penny began crying, too.

Charlie kept his arm about her waist as he turned to face the preacher. "I take this woman to be my lawfully wedded wife."

"And I take this man to be my lawfully wedded husband," she added, beaming up at him.

Reverend Hammond closed his Bible, his dark eyes danced with amusement. "Then I think it's safe to say, I can now pronounce you man and wife."

Charlie bent over and kissed her with a firm, but gentle pressure. The kind of kiss that sealed his love and his vows.

When he straightened, she took a deep breath. Her feet couldn't be on the floor because she was certain she was floating.

Only one more thing remained to be done. Penny reached for his hand and gave him the ornament, a symbol of their mutual love and commitment. "The drum rightfully belongs over there. Why don't you put it with the others you placed on the tree?"

"Good idea." Charlie stepped around the preacher, who didn't look nearly as surprised as everyone else did, and hung the drum ornament next to the partridge.

"You sly dog," Reverend Hammond murmured. "What got you in the Christmas spirit?"

Charlie gave a shrug, as if he hadn't given it a thought. Only, Penny knew better. "Twelve days, twelve gifts. Hey, somebody ought to write a song about that."

SERIES EPILOGUE

JANUARY 6, 1877, NOELLE, COLORADO

"*I* hereby call this meeting to order." Charlie pounded a gavel on the table where he and Chase Hammond, along with their wives and three representatives from the Denver & Pacific Railroad, were seated. Other townsfolk were gathered at nearby tables situated around the saloon. The Golden Nugget served as a church and wedding venue, so why not a town hall?

Charlie picked up an official document he'd signed off on yesterday. The town had delivered on their promise, now it was up to the railroad board to agree to a date when construction would start on the new railroad line, and as mayor, he intended to close this deal *today*.

"Back in the summer, we made an agreement with the railroad's land agent, Percival Penworthy, which called for twelve married couples to be presented no later than January sixth." Charlie glanced over at Chase, and his best friend—the town's one and only preacher, who'd dreamed up the marriage scheme—winked at him. Chase knew full well how close they'd come to blowing this deadline —quite literally with that mine explosion the day before.

"In attendance are the following couples," Charlie read from the certified list. "Reverend and Mrs. Hammond, Mr. and Mrs. Daniels…"

Culver and Zee stood. The grin on the man's face as he held a chubby six-month old was evidence enough he'd taken to fatherhood surprisingly fast, considering baby Jemimah had been a complete surprise—to everyone.

"Mr. and Mrs. Burnside, Mr. and Mrs. Peregrine, Sheriff Draven and his missus…" As Charlie called their names, the couples seated around the tables stood briefly. "Mr. and Mrs. Thornton—"

Loud honks came from beneath the table where Storm and Molly were seated. Storm's grandpa Ezra reached down to pat the head of an enormous gander snuggled up next to a smaller goose. "Yes, you too, Daniel. We didn't forget you and your missus."

Restraining a laugh, Charlie continued: "Mr. and Mrs. Fulton, Mr. and Mrs. Deane, Mr. and Mrs. Villanueva, Mr. and Mrs. Montgomery, Mr. and Mrs. Kinnison, and you all have met my wife, Mrs. Hardt."

Charlie slipped his arm around Penny's waist after she stood up. He still could hardly believe his good fortune. His *good luck* Penny. "We're here today to certify these marriages met the deadline imposed by the agent for the railroad. All twelve couples were legally wed before midnight. In return, we expect the railroad board to commit to a *firm* date for when construction will begin."

"Hear, hear!" Seamus shouted. The barkeeper gave Charlie a thumbs-up. He'd admitted to being so overcome by all the weddings, he had sent for his estranged wife who lived out East, in hopes she'd come West and they could reconcile.

Just as Charlie had predicted, things were starting to turn around, and Noelle's future looked bright indeed. He felt good about their chances for sealing this deal. Besides meeting the deadline, they'd also just discovered a fortune in silver and the lead containing it was just waiting to be dug out of the original mine he'd started five years earlier. *Thank*

God. The mountain had made it clear enough it would yield little more gold. Besides, the entrance to the gold mine had collapsed after being rigged with explosives, and it would cost too much to salvage it. Now the trick would be coming up with enough money to extract the silver, an expensive proposition.

The three railroad officials at the table didn't return Charlie's smile. That was the first clue they might be in trouble.

"Very nice speech, Mayor Hardt." One of the railroad officials remarked in a dry tone. The gentleman had introduced himself as Mr. Stiles—the *real* Mr. Stiles, not the imposter sitting in the town jail who had nearly killed Pearl because of some crazy mix-up. Charlie didn't much like this Mr. Stiles either. "Before we get started, our president has something to say."

Of course he did. Gaylord Penworthy couldn't be too happy about the fact his nephew, Percival, was also being held in the town's jail, awaiting formal charges that he'd conspired with the man who'd blown up the gold mine, and, very nearly, Charlie with it. Wary, Charlie set the gavel aside. "You have the floor, sir."

Penworthy stood, tugging at his coat to adjust it over his protruding stomach, which, along with the bushy muttonchops and heavy eyebrows gave him the appearance of an annoyed badger. He was only slighter taller than he was wide, while his nephew had the build of a beanpole. Uncle Gaylord should've shared his meals with Percy.

"We're aware of the unfortunate situation involving the fraudulent claim on your mine, Mr. Hardt, and I understand your concerns. But I can assure you, our land agent had no knowledge of any wrongdoing, and Percival had nothing whatsoever to do with that unfortunate explosion." The railroad owner's defense didn't surprise Charlie. After all, Percy was his nephew. That didn't mean he'd get a pass.

Thus far, the sheriff had pieced together enough evidence to show that Charlie's former partner, George Cortland, had—ironically—died in an explosion he'd set in order to get Charlie out of the way before declaring ownership in the gold mine and selling out to the railroad. How much Percy knew about the attempted murder was hard to say. But it was too soon to declare him innocent. As was right and proper, a jury would decide his fate.

But what if Percy's uncle had been in on the plan to gain control of the gold mine? That possibility loomed large, and Charlie wasn't so naïve he hadn't considered it, and how this might impact Noelle's chances with the railroad. The inscrutable expressions on the faces of the other two railroad representatives gave nothing away. Maybe they were *all* in on it.

Charlie tensed, as anger rolled over him in a hot wave. Penny's light touch on his wrist served as a reminder to keep his cool. Her calm demeanor centered him, and he took a deep breath before answering. "You'll have ample opportunity, sir, to provide testimony on your nephew's behalf. We will abide by the decision of the court."

Penny's serene expression shifted only slightly. Not enough that anyone other than Charlie would notice, still, he could tell she was pleased with his measured response. She was so good for him, and he intended to be good for her, too...more than good. He wanted to place the world at her feet. And now, with all that silver, he had a chance.

After a brief hesitation, Penworthy acquiesced with a nod. "Yes, well, the courts will, of course, decide the matter. In the meantime, we'll be assigning a new land agent." He gestured to another well-fed gentleman on his right. "This is Mr. Solomon Sharp, from Philadelphia."

Charlie tried not to let disappointment show on his face. *Another Easterner.* Why couldn't they pick someone local? Storm Thornton would make a good land agent, if he were interested in the job. He had impeccable integrity as well as the respect of the entire town.

Solomon Sharp stood with a small, tight smile. "Very pleased to make your acquaintance. I'm looking forward to my time in Noelle. From what I've already seen, I can tell this is a, um, delightful place, ripe with possibilities. We're very eager to hear more about this silver strike."

Ripe for the picking, he meant. These shysters couldn't wait to get their hands on that silver. "First, let's get the date for the construction of the railroad line settled, then we can talk about silver," Charlie replied in an even tone.

Penworthy laced his fingers over his chest and his frown deepened. "Mayor Hardt, we understand that your gold mine is, at present, inaccessible, and currently is not producing much gold. *Gold* was the reason the railroad agreed to come through here in the first place. We have the right to know whether our investment will pay off."

Of course Charlie knew gold was the reason the railroad was interested. He'd known that all along. But he'd assumed, wrongly perhaps, that the railroad board would be encouraged enough by the prospect of silver to move ahead. Plus, the town had met the marriage deadline per their agreement. Although it was obvious now, the marriage agreement Percy got behind had only been intended as a distraction from his underhanded dealings, and his uncle wasn't above welshing on the deal.

Charlie also knew he'd have to handle this situation carefully if they were to have a chance at securing the railroad line, which was absolutely necessary for the town's survival. "We've known for some time that our mountain had large quantities of lead. How much silver we can extract from it still needs to be determined. After that, we can elaborate."

"What's that? *Celebrate?* Are we having another party?" The exclamation came from the Peregrines' table, where Jack and Birdie sat with Jack's grandfather, Gus, and an elderly woman who'd arrived in town with the other brides.

Old Gus darted a surprised look around. "Who's gettin' hitched now?"

Agatha Boonesbury bumped him with her elbow. "*We* are, old man. Later today. Don't you remember?"

Gus winked at his *girl*, who had to be seventy if she was a day. "Sure I do! Took me three tries to stand up after I went down on one knee."

Agatha gathered her betrothed's gnarled fingers.

"As I remember, you jumped up and gave me a big—"

"Mr. Hardt was talking about silver," the new land agent blurted.

Gus slapped his hand on the table. "Well, I'll be. Did somebody get us a silver service?"

Grandpa Gus could be hard of hearing at times, but Charlie suspected Gus knew exactly what he was about at the moment—distracting the railroad officials from a discussion about the silver mine.

"It appears to me, we have *thirteen* couples, Mr. Penworthy," Chase pointed out. "As you can see, we're a growing town. We've been hauling gold out of *The Drum* for three years straight, and soon we'll be hauling out silver. What more is there to say? Let's get this line built!"

"Amen! You tell 'em, preacher!" shouted Woody Burnside. His Chinese wife beamed at him. Meizhen didn't say much, but it was pretty clear she didn't need to. Everyone knew how she felt about Woody.

She petted a chicken resting contentedly in her lap. Two other hens roosted near Woody's chair. Chickens were supposed to be stupid, but those three... Well, they behaved more like dogs.

"Your company will need a backer to go after all that silver," Penworthy pointed out to Charlie. "It won't be cheap to mine the ore, much less build a smelter."

Charlie considered telling *Uncle G* to go hang. Everything the cussed cur said was true. Nonetheless, Charlie would prefer to cut a deal with Old Scratch rather than sell out to this scoundrel. "It's too early to talk about that right now."

"Nonsense, this is the perfect time, and I'm in a position to offer you the full backing of the Denver & Pacific Railroad. We'll strike a deal, finish this line and get that silver rolling all at the same time." Penworthy tucked his thumbs beneath his lapels and his false smile turned smug.

Charlie didn't like being backed into a corner any better than Bandit did. Unlike the ferret, he couldn't show his fangs.

Penny shifted forward wearing an innocent expression. "Oh dear, Mr. Penworthy, perhaps I heard wrong, but are you saying you intend to *dishonor* an agreement made in good faith with the honest citizens of this town?"

Minnie Montgomery gasped and put her hand to her chest. "Why, I believe that's *exactly* what he's saying. My father will be surprised, and very disappointed, to hear this."

"As will mine," Felicity Hammond chimed in.

"Father doesn't look kindly on men who break their promises"

The two Denver socialites, whose fathers were big investors in the railroad, knew what they were about, as did Penny. Charlie reached beneath the table and clasped her hand in gratitude. She squeezed his fingers. They might never be able to prove that dishonest old badger was involved in his nephew's scheme, but they could besmirch his reputation, which would be almost as bad.

Penworthy's face darkened. Now who felt cornered? "You ladies have it all wrong. I'm only pointing out that your town won't be producing silver if Mr. Hardt's company can't afford to mine it. Railroad money can help the silver mine become operational, which, of course, will ensure the town's survival. Unless Mr. Hardt already has the funds?"

Charlie's momentary satisfaction faded. He'd committed the majority of his resources on a futile search for more gold and couldn't guarantee he had enough remaining capital to get the silver mine up and running. Not yet, but he would find a way.

"A moment, if you please." Felicity stood and looked around the room, expectantly. "I think we townsfolk should have the first chance to invest in the silver mine."

Investors? Oh no, no more partners. Not after what

happened the last time.

But this was Chase and Felicity. Charlie knew he could trust his friends, who also happened to be as poor as church mice. Where would they get the funds?

Looking alarmed, Chase grabbed his wife's elbow and drew her down to whisper something in her ear. Her mouth formed an O, but then she spoke, just loud enough for others to hear: "Yes, dear. We have a little money stashed away. I might've forgotten to mention that trust from my grandmother." She gave Chase an apologetic smile and kiss on the cheek. "I'm sure you don't mind if we invest it in Charlie's mine."

Chase shook his head, looking a little stunned. "No...no, I don't mind."

The smitten preacher would agree to anything his wife asked. Charlie knew the feeling well.

"Thank you. That's a nice gesture." Charlie couldn't refuse to let his best friend invest in the mine, even if it happened to be with his wife's money.

Hugh Montgomery lifted his hand. "We'd be pleased to invest."

His wife Minnie nodded enthusiastically. "Oh yes, whatever you need."

Charlie nodded, still a little stunned. He could

take a second, small investment from the assayer and his wife and still maintain control.

"Just a moment," Zeke Kinnison called out. He turned to his wife, the former matchmaker, Genevieve Walters. "I think it may be time to invest in something more permanent since we plan to stay."

"I wholeheartedly agree." Genevieve smiled and hugged his arm. "My uncle will be interested in investing, as well. And it's also a good time to begin work on the women's mission that Penny and I wish to start in Noelle."

"That's a grand idea, Genevieve!" Penny gushed. "Don't you think so, Charlie?"

"Wonderful...yeah." It was a grand idea, and Charlie couldn't refuse Zeke, knowing how much courage it took for him to come off that mountain and rejoin the living.

"Well then, I'd like to throw in a little cash, too." Woody looked at Charlie, questioningly. "Is that all right with you, Mr. Hardt?"

Charlie couldn't turn Woody down. His employee and friend had been unswerving in his loyalty over the years. "It's all right with me."

The three hens began to cackle and Woody laughed. "Mimi, Fifi and Gigi think it's a good idea, too."

"Hens with ideas? Preposterous!" Stiles sat up with a scowl. "Now see here, this mine will belong to the railroad—er, I mean, to Mr. Hardt *and* the railroad."

Charlie pinned the *real* Mr. Stiles with a hard stare. "I never said I would—"

"Why does the *railroad* get first dibs?" Culver Daniels called out from his seat "They aren't even here yet."

"That's right. We're the ones invested in this town." Liam Fulton took his wife's hand and drew her forward. "Mayor, me and Avis, we want to invest in your mine."

"*Si*, we wish to put some money in, as well," Nacho Villanueva chimed in.

His wife Josefina slipped her arm through his. "If owning part of a silver mine helps finance a search for my sister, I'm in agreement."

"Mayor, count us in." Jack Peregrine put his hand on his grandfather's shoulder and covered Birdie's small hand. "All three of us."

"Four!" Gus reached his arm around the back of his betrothed's chair. "Aggie's in, too."

More offers came from Doc Deane and Cara, then Storm Thornton and Molly. Even the geese put in their two-cents—or two honks, as it were.

Draven slipped off the stool at the bar and

hugged Pearl close. "What the hell, might as well add our names to the list so I can afford to buy her some nice baubles."

Charlie could hardly catch his breath as the offers came in, fast and furious. He didn't know quite how to answer. As much as he appreciated their good intentions and didn't want to refuse, accepting their money meant relinquishing something he wasn't sure he could give up quite so easily.

"Charlie?" Penny searched his face with confusion, and then awareness dawned in her eyes, followed by empathy. She leaned close and spoke in a low voice. "I know what the mine means to you, and I know it's hard to let go, but this town has people who love Noelle as much as you do. Let them help us save it."

She understood him so well. In fact, she understood him better than he understood himself. Absolution wasn't an easy thing to come by. God knew how intensely he'd sought it, even to the point of creating something he could pour his life into in order to make up for what he hadn't been able to give his child. But this town wasn't his child, and Penny—sweet, insightful Penny—she'd seen through him again, and she was right. He'd held on to the mines and clung to his control over the town because he was afraid to let go and risk losing everything. Again.

Except, he wouldn't lose everything. He had Penny. Besides, she was right; the people assembled here had stepped up to save Noelle, and they deserved to partake in the mine's, as well as the town's, success. Hadn't she already said the mine belonged to Noelle? This just made it official.

Charlie faced the railroad officials whose greed threatened their future. "As much as I appreciate the railroad's offer, it looks like we have enough investors to get started, so we won't need additional funds."

Penworthy glanced at the other officials, who appeared at a loss for words. Then again, they might be leaving the decision up to him. He could either make good on his nephew's promise or risk alienating two important investors in Denver.

After a long moment, Penworthy gave a disgruntled sigh. "All right then, you'll have your railroad line. We'll start construction in the spring."

Amidst triumphant shouts and clapping, Charlie reached for the affidavit and drew a pen from the inkwell, holding it out. "If you'll sign here..."

The End...or is it?

AUTHOR'S NOTE

The mail-order bride phenomenon in 19th century America spawned personal advertisements, matrimonial newspapers and matchmaking services. The inspiration for *Twelve Days of Christmas Mail-Order Brides,* however, came from the brilliant mind of USA Today bestselling author Caroline Lee—after a dream!

Our series is set in the fictional town of Noelle, Colorado, which is loosely based on the actual history of Leadville. That gold mining community had nearly petered out until silver was discovered, almost by accident. After that, the town exploded, becoming one of the richest and wildest western

American towns in existence at the end of the 19th century.

I'm so grateful to Caroline Lee for inviting me along on this journey, and what a fun trip we've taken together, along with ten other bestselling authors. I've thoroughly enjoyed brainstorming this series and then seeing how each author took their couple's love story and blended it into the overall tale about a little town named after a baby.

I hope you'll enjoy reading about Noelle and the twelve couples determined to save it.

Merrily,
    E.E. Burke

ABOUT THE AUTHOR

E.E. Burke is a bestselling author of emotionally powerful historical and contemporary romances that combine her unique blend of wit and warmth. Her books have been nominated for numerous national and regional awards, including Booksellers' Best, National Readers' Choice and Kindle Best Book. She was also a finalist in the RWA's prestigious Golden Heart® contest. Over the years, she's been a disc jockey, a journalist and an advertising executive, before finally getting around to living the dream-- writing stories readers can get lost in.

The Brides of Noelle

Jolie, Valentine's Day Bride

The Bride Train Series

Valentine's Rose

Patrick's Charm

Tempting Prudence

Seducing Susannah

American Mail-Order Brides

Victoria, Bride of Kansas

Santa's Mail-Order Bride
Also in audiobook

Steam! Romance and Rails Series
Her Bodyguard
Kate's Outlaw
A Dangerous Passion
Fugitive Hearts

Texas Hardts
Maybe Baby

Receive a FREE book when you sign up for my
newsletter at www.eeburke.com